"Kerry, we have to be sensible about this. I'm not going to dangle you out there like a Judas goat."

"But that's what I am. Or I should be." She leaned back against the cushions, closing her eyes. "I'm not afraid of dying."

"No," Adrian said. "Has it occurred to you that I might be afraid of losing you?"

"Adrian…" She couldn't bring herself to open her eyes. Her heart seemed to stop midbeat, and the breath sailed out of her.

"Just don't argue with me, Kerry. Just don't argue. I know you're bait. But none of us, me most especially, is willing to risk you recklessly. You've got to understand that."

At that she opened her eyes and looked at him, reading the urgency in his face, the deep concern, even the flicker of fear. She understood that it would kill him to lose someone he was protecting again. Almost as if to reinforce his message, he swept her up off the couch and carried her back to her bedroom.

Dear Reader,

I've changed over the years, and as a result there had to be some changes to CONARD COUNTY, too. I think you'll find that the things you love most are still in these pages, but we have a younger generation now, with our old favorites still turning up.

This younger generation has a slightly different spin on the world, and so for only the second time I am introducing the element of the paranormal in *Protector of One*. But you know what? I've lived in a haunted house, I went through periods of precognition and ESP that were astonishing when I was younger, so why not bring them into the lives of people in Conard County? I hope you enjoy reading about them as much as I enjoyed writing about them.

At heart, as always, these are stories about the triumph of love. Because it is love that gives meaning to our days, and purpose to our lives. It is love that helps us through the trying times, and gives us the greatest joy we will ever know.

Join me at my Web site devoted to Conard County, www.conardcounty.com, to let me know what you think and what you'd like to read. Your opinions matter greatly.

Hugs,

Rachel

RACHEL LEE

Protector of One

Silhouette®

Romantic
SUSPENSE

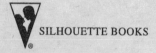 SILHOUETTE BOOKS

Recycling programs
for this product may
not exist in your area.

ISBN-13: 978-0-373-27625-7
ISBN-10:   0-373-27625-7

PROTECTOR OF ONE

Copyright © 2009 by Susan Civil Brown

RACHEL LEE

was hooked on writing by the age of twelve, and practiced her craft as she moved from place to place all over the United States. This *New York Times* bestselling author now resides in Florida and has the joy of writing full-time.

Her bestselling CONARD COUNTY series has won the hearts of readers worldwide, and it's no wonder, given her own approach to life and love. As she says, "Life is the biggest romantic adventure of all—and if you're open and aware, the most marvelous things are just waiting to be discovered."

For all my readers, each and every one,
who help me keep Conard County alive.
Hugs to you all!

Prologue

It was a dark and stormy night. The most clichéd opening line in literature should have been the start of the story, Kerry Tomlinson would later think. As an English teacher she had used the line often to instruct.

In reality, it was a bright and sunny autumn morning, redolent of coffee, sizzling bacon and the nutty aroma of grits and cheese. In the background, the radio played some lively but pleasant music. She sat at her table with the *Conard County Courier* open in front of her, waiting for the strip of bacon she intended to crumble into the steaming bowl of grits beside the stove.

She heard the newsbreak start, the report of two

bodies being found on the edge of the state forest in Conard County, two hikers...

Then her world turned upside down.

Chapter 1

Adrian Goddard sat in Conard County Sheriff Gage Dalton's Office, about as unhappy as a man could be short of death or major injury. He'd left law enforcement two years ago and he wasn't happy to be dragged back in. But a double homicide had caused Gage to call on him, and his sense of duty wouldn't let him refuse.

A lean, rangy man with a face marked by weather and strain, his gray eyes pierced whatever he looked at and nearly matched the early gray at his temples. He looked as if he might have been chiseled out of the granite of the Wyoming mountains. He had one of those faces that made guessing his age nearly impossible, yet few would have believed he was only thirty-five.

He'd spent the day at the crime scene, gathering the kind of information a photograph or a report might overlook: angles of attack, best vantage points, surrounding cover. The little and big things that could answer the question: why did this happen here and not elsewhere? Given the relative isolation of the wooded murder scene, that question had gained a lot of importance.

Gage returned to the office, looking as tired as any man who'd spent the day looking at two partially decomposed bodies while marching up and down rocky ground looking for footprints and cartridge casings. Maybe worse than tired, because Gage lived his life in constant pain, the only outward signs of which were his limp and the burn scar on his cheek and neck.

"Nate's going to come in tomorrow," Gage said.

"Good," Adrian answered. Nate Tate was the former sheriff of Conard County. He'd retired a couple of years ago to be succeeded by Gage Dalton, a man still referred to as "the new sheriff." But Adrian had worked more often with Nate over the years than he had with Gage, so he knew the man's mettle and doubted anyone on the planet knew this county better. If anybody in Conard County had a screw loose, Nate would know who it was and would probably even have the guy's phone number memorized. A good starting place in a case like this.

Gage settled in his chair, a pillow behind his back, reflexive pain showing only in a minute tightening around his dark eyes. "Okay," he said, "we're getting nowhere fast. We should probably call it a night."

"Probably." Oddly, however, Adrian felt reluctant to return to the peace of his ranch. The place he had chosen to be his hermitage. His fortress.

"I don't get it," he said. "Was it a hate killing? It looks like it. The way these guys were arranged...."

Gage winced again, this time at the thought. "I don't want a Matthew Shepard thing in this county."

"Who does? But it doesn't feel right anyway. You saw them. Something about it keeps nagging at me. Misdirection. That's what I'm thinking."

Gage nodded, pulling a couple of the crime scene photos toward him. "I guess we won't know for sure until we find out who they are."

Any identifiable items had been removed. Adrian stared at a photo, thinking. "If it was a hate crime, wouldn't they want us to know who the vics are?"

"You're talking about a rational mind, Adrian."

"Even neo-Nazis can be rational. They're just *wrong*."

At that a faint smile flickered over Gage's face. "Maybe."

"Well, the statement gets kind of overlooked if it takes us weeks to find out who these guys are. By then the news will have moved on."

"Don't mention the news. The major media are going to crawl all over us tomorrow." Gage heaved a resigned sigh.

"Too bad," Adrian said, "that these guys couldn't have been on state forest land."

"Yeah. Then we could have called in your old buddies."

Adrian had retired on disability from the Wyoming

Department of Criminal Investigation. He would have loved to turn all of this over to them.

Or maybe not. Despite himself, his interest was piqued.

"Too bad," Gage said, "it didn't happen in Denver. Anywhere but my county."

"Gage?"

At the soft voice both men looked up to see Emma Dalton, Gage's wife, standing in the doorway. The years had dissolved none of her beauty, and to Gage she still appeared to be the redheaded, green-eyed goddess he'd fallen in love with in the darkest time of both their lives. "Have you got time to listen to a witness?"

"Witness to what?"

"The murders. Kerry Tomlinson. You remember her. She had a vision about it."

The two men looked at each other, neither of them knowing what to make of this announcement. It was almost as if they had just ridden over the hump in a roller coaster, the word *witness* starting to fill them with excitement just as the word *vision* sent them plunging. But there was Emma, a paragon if ever there was one, asking them to listen.

Gage cleared his throat. "I didn't know Kerry was a psychic."

"She's not." Emma stepped into the room and closed the door behind her. She smelled like rose water and the library, and a touch of cold autumn air. "But she's very scared and very frightened, and she can't shake the images out of her mind. So you are going to listen to her and reassure her. If she's got information you can use, good. If not you can at least put her mind to rest about whether she's really seeing the murder victims."

Gage and Adrian exchanged looks again. To Adrian it seemed both of them felt the same reluctance.

"Okay," Gage answered after a moment. "But we're not shrinks. Let me just put all this stuff out of sight."

Emma glanced down and her lips tightened. "Please do," she said. "I don't need to look at that, either. Let me get her."

Emma hovered over her like a guardian angel, Kerry thought as they walked down the hall to the sheriff's office. The sense of having an ally in this craziness reassured her almost as much as the sense of an unseen presence just behind her shoulder disturbed her. Emma might spread her metaphoric wings, but those wings seemed unable to hold back the push from the invisible presence.

This is insane.

But insane or not, she had the strong feeling that if she didn't spit out these images, they were going to plague her forever.

She entered Gage's office tentatively, giving him a small, weak smile. Then she saw the other man. Tall, rugged-looking, dark hair with a dash of gray at the temples. Adrian Goddard. What was he doing here?

At that instant she almost turned and ran. Being crazy was one thing. Announcing it to a whole bunch of people, one of them almost a stranger, was entirely another. His gray eyes flicked over her, as full of doubt as any atheist's when inside a church.

"I can't do this!" The words burst from her and she started to turn, but Emma gently caught her arm.

"You can," Emma said firmly. "None of us know what happened to you this morning. Nobody can say whether it was something random occurring because of the news you heard, or whether you really saw something. But one thing I *do* know, Kerry. You're not crazy, and if there's even a slender hope that you might have picked up on something useful, you owe it to the victims to tell Gage."

Kerry closed her eyes a moment, felt again the pressure pushing her forward, thought she almost heard a whisper in her ear. "Okay," she said, squaring her shoulders. "Maybe if I tell you all, I can forget about it, which would be a blessing."

She took one of the two chairs facing the desk, refusing to look at Adrian Goddard. Right now she needed his apparent dubiousness as much as she needed another vision. Gage merely looked inquiring. And kind.

"It's okay, Kerry," he said. "Before this week is out we'll have had a handful of people claim to have committed these murders even though they had nothing to do with them, and a thousand useless tips. And we have no leads at this point. So a vision of any kind is welcome, okay?"

Kerry nodded slowly, trying to find the persona that could control a classroom full of rowdy teens, and leave behind the disturbed woman she had become today.

"Okay," she said. "Okay." But it was going to be one of the hardest things she'd ever done.

Adrian leaned back in his chair, folding his hands on his flat stomach, trying to appear impassive. His gaze bored into Kerry Tomlinson, though. A schoolteacher with visions. He'd noticed her around, of course. You couldn't live in Conard County for long without noticing just about everyone.

She was tiny, almost frail-looking, with long dark hair caught in a clip at the nape of her neck. Her dark eyes were large in her face, her cheekbones high and her unpainted lips invitingly shaped. Pretty, but able to pass unnoticed if she chose. A quiet prettiness, the kind that for the right person could easily turn into brilliant beauty. A man would have to approach carefully, slowly, and gently, to bring that out, but once he did...

Catching himself, Adrian almost shook his head to bring his attention back to what she was saying.

"It's hard to explain," she said, looking at Gage. "I was just sitting there waiting for my breakfast to finish cooking..." She trailed off and looked down at her knotted hands.

"Start wherever you want," Gage said gently. "You don't have to get right to the vision."

That seemed to reassure her. Her head lifted, and Adrian now saw the woman who taught for a living, the woman who could handle rooms full of teenagers.

"All right," she said, her voice taking on a somewhat stronger timbre. "When I was in my senior year in college, we were driving back to school after the holidays when the car skidded on ice and went over a cliff. My two friends died. Probably the only reason I'm still here is that I was in the backseat, and an EMT saw us go off the road."

Gage nodded, didn't ask her how this was related. Just let her tell her story her own way, which was often the best way.

"Anyway," Kerry continued, "I died twice."

In spite of himself, Adrian sat up a little straighter. Gage leaned forward and repeated, *"Twice?"*

Kerry nodded. "That's what they tell me. I was clinically dead twice before they managed to stabilize me. I'm lucky not to have suffered major brain damage."

"I would say so!" Gage agreed heartily.

A faint smile flickered over Kerry's face. "I'll spare you the tale about going into the light. My near-death experience was pretty much the same as everyone's you hear about. *I* know it was real. I don't need to convince anyone else."

Gage nodded. Adrian sat frozen. He would have liked to demand the details for himself, but held on to his desire. Another time. A better time.

"Anyway," Kerry said, "I recovered, I finished school, I came back here to teach. You all know the rest. I've been teaching here for eight years now," she added to Adrian, as if he might not know. "But I changed after the accident."

"Most people do," Emma said comfortingly. She would know. A senseless, brutal crime had once torn her life apart.

Kerry looked at her and nodded gratefully. "Anyway," she continued, returning her attention to Gage, "everything checked out, not even any brain damage that they could find. I was lucky. I was blessed."

Gage murmured agreement. Adrian could tell that Kerry didn't really feel blessed and suspected some survivor guilt. She'd be less than human if she didn't feel it.

Kerry drew a deep breath, clearly ready to plunge in to the hard part. "I sometimes get these feelings. I call them my quirks. But sometimes I know things that are going to happen. Or I know things that happen elsewhere that I only hear about later. I usually shake them off. Coincidence. Probably the result of some minor brain damage."

Gage nodded. "Possibly."

"But this morning..." Kerry hesitated. Finally she closed her eyes, as if to pretend she were alone, and said, "I heard the news announcement and then everything just shifted. In an instant I was somewhere else and the things I saw were all jumbled."

Gage leaned forward now, picking up a pen and holding it over a legal pad. "Can you organize it in any way?"

Kerry compressed her lips before speaking. "It was like a rush of things, disjointed, some not clear, others almost too clear. Sounds. I heard men laughing. I heard them opening cans, and could smell the beer. I smelled cordite. I saw...I saw... I saw two men lying on the ground. They were facing each other, and each had an arm over the other's body. And blood. There was blood every-where... They were shot. Twice each. Once in the chest, once in the head. But they weren't lying like that when they were shot. They were dragged there. Positioned."

Her eyes snapped open. "It's supposed to look like a message, but it's not."

That was the moment Adrian felt the hairs on the back of his neck stand on end.

Kerry waited, but she hardly saw Gage and Adrian now. She had returned to this morning, that bright beautiful morning that had been suddenly and inexplicably blighted by evil. At some level she smelled the bacon burning on the stove, but her mind had attached itself far away from the kitchen.

"Kerry?" Gage's voice recalled her.

"Yes?"

"Can you wring any more details out of what you sensed?"

She met his gaze and saw something there, something that suggested she hadn't just flipped a brain circuit. "You mean what I saw was real?"

Emma squeezed her arm again. Gage hesitated. "I'm not supposed to discuss the investigation. So can we just say that you hit on something that no one outside the department should know?"

"Oh, God." Kerry lowered her head, her stomach sinking at the same time. "I don't need this. I don't want this...this whatever it is."

"I don't blame you," Emma said quietly. "But for whatever reason, it happened."

Kerry nodded, fighting for equilibrium and battering down the fright. "Okay. Okay. Let's just say that somehow, some way, I saw something that was real. At least in part. You want me to try to wring more information out of what I saw?"

"If you can."

"It was all so jumbled, and I've been trying not to think about it all day." Her fingers twisted together. "Let me think. Focus on it. But at this point I'm not sure I wouldn't just confabulate stuff."

"Wouldn't it feel different?" Adrian asked, speaking for the first time.

Kerry looked at him, her jaw dropping a little. "Yes," she said finally. "It would. There was something about what happened this morning that was so...real. Almost hyper-real."

He nodded. "Then don't worry about making things up. Just focus on what feels like that."

"Good idea," Gage remarked.

Kerry decided that would make a good guideline. Somewhere through her distress a flicker of humor emerged. "I'm not a pro at this. No practice to guide me."

At that even the stern-faced Adrian smiled. "I've never consulted a psychic before so I don't have any hints for you."

"I'm not a psychic. I just—" She broke off suddenly. "Sorry. It doesn't matter what I am or am not. Whatever this was, it happened. So I just need to make sure I tell you everything."

Gage nodded encouragingly. "That's the stuff. Then maybe you can go home and forget it."

"That would be a relief. All right." She closed her eyes again, this time not trying to skip quickly through the images that had imprinted themselves earlier that day, but instead to look hard at them.

"The victims were friends. One of them—there's a woman starting to worry about him. A young woman. She wants to report him missing."

"That'll help," Adrian said.

Kerry ignored him, reaching out into whatever it was that had happened this morning, unsure but driven to find something, anything that would get this off her back and help the police if she could.

"They'd been on a long hike," she said. "Getting near the end. Several days, maybe a week. I see a camera. A camera was important to one of them. And a funny-looking hammer. They both had these hammers on their belts before they were killed. The murderer took them, and some other things."

Where was all this coming from? But the words kept tumbling from her lips, sometimes fast, sometimes hesitant. "There's more than one murderer," she announced suddenly. "I get the feeling of competition. This won't be the last killing."

Then it was as if a bubble burst. Everything drained from her mind, leaving her relaxed. Whatever she had needed to do was done now. Finished.

She opened her eyes again, looking at the two men. "That's it. It's gone."

"Gone?" Gage asked.

"Gone. The vividness is gone. It's just like any memory now."

Emma spoke. "That's good. Now you're free of it."

Kerry poked around inside her own head as if she were using her tongue to find a sore tooth. "Yes," she said presently. "It's gone." And with it all the pressure that had been working on her all day. Gone, too, was the sense of a presence. All of it, gone, and for the first time since the news had come on that morning, she felt like her old self.

"Thank God," she said. A long sigh escaped her and she started to smile. "All right, that's it. I told you. I hope it helps, but I'm done with it now."

Gage rose and reached to shake her hand. "Thanks, Kerry. I appreciate it. You *did* help."

Chapter 2

Fifteen minutes later, Kerry closed the front door of her house behind her and locked it. Home surrounded her with welcoming familiarity. The smell of burned bacon still clouded the air, however, and she immediately headed for the kitchen to clean up the mess she'd left behind. The congealed grits still sat beside the stove, now in a condition to be used for glue. The blackened strip of bacon looked like a desiccated finger. All of it went into the garbage disposal, and the dishes to soak in hot soapy water.

She used a can of air freshener throughout the house, spraying it freely, because the smell of burned bacon kept trying to carry her back to that morning. She had to get rid of it. Soon a lemony scent had erased the reminder.

From the freezer she chose a prepackaged dinner because she didn't feel like cooking today. Ordinarily she made herself do it because it was healthier, but cooking for one was rarely fun, and tonight she just couldn't face it.

Something in her had changed today, she realized as she carried her microwaved dinner into the living room and reached for the TV remote. Ordinarily she didn't notice the silence of her house, but she was feeling it now, oppressively. Usually she picked up a book, not the TV remote, and only if she didn't have papers to grade.

She had a stack of essays waiting for her, plenty of books nearby, but she needed the companionship of sound, even the manufactured sounds of television. She chose a nature program about birds—the sound of their songs felt cheerful—and tried to focus on the narrator's voice only to discover a gloomy description of the decreasing number of birds in the U.S.

Maybe she'd assign an essay on conservation or the environment next week. Or maybe not. Reaching for the remote, she began flipping through channels seeking anything that would shake the cloud of murk that seemed to have descended.

In the end, though, she quit trying to distract herself. The vision may have loosened its grip, but the fact that it had occurred remained a problem. Instead of looking at this morning's experience directly, though, she chose instead to move back in time, to the moment when she had, as they said, "touched the light."

She'd read all the explanations of the experience,

from both the scientific and religious sides. But none of it could erase or in any way diminish her experience. As much as she had loved in her life, she had never known a love like *that*. Just remembering it still had the power to leave her feeling homesick, the only word she could think of that even approached the yearning she felt for that moment out of time.

Nor could anyone or anything convince her that that love wasn't waiting for her when she died the final time.

She had managed to fit that life-altering experience into herself and her being, and used it as a touchstone, a constant reminder of what she owed her fellow humans, the world as a whole.

But now this. What the hell had happened this morning? Now that she was free of its stranglehold, she needed to explain it somehow. Deal with it. Find a way to slip it into the defined realm of possibilities in her life. Most people weren't comfortable with loose ends and she certainly wasn't.

Apparently, from the reaction she had received—unless Gage and Adrian had been indulging her—she had said something that got their attention. But what did it *mean?*

The sound of the front doorbell replaced silence with cheerful promise. She and her friends observed an "open-door" policy. Nobody needed an invitation or to make a phone call before dropping in.

But when she opened the door, she found not one of her friends, but instead Adrian Goddard. The sight so startled her that she didn't greet him immediately.

"Sorry to drop by like this," he said. "Do you have a minute to talk?"

"Sure," she said after a moment's hesitation. Stepping back, she allowed him to come inside, along with a gust of cold air.

"Winter's not far away," he remarked with a smile that didn't reach his eyes.

"No, but this is my favorite time of year. Autumn is special. Would you like coffee or something?"

"No thanks. I don't want to impose. Just a brief chat."

She nodded and led him to the living room, wincing as she saw her solitary, hardly touched meal still sitting on the coffee table. Talk about revealing!

He settled on one end of the couch at her invitation, and she took the rocking chair that faced him kitty-corner. She reached for the remote and then shut off the TV.

"This isn't official or anything," he told her. In fact, she thought he looked awkward. "I was thinking as I was getting ready to drive home. How hard this must have been for you. What you saw, and having to tell us, then our reaction to it. I just wanted to make sure you're all right."

"All right?" She looked at the table with the microwave tray on it, at the glass of milk beside it, at the TV remote she had reached for because tonight she needed some kind of companionship. She could have called a friend, but that would have meant discussing this morning, the last thing she felt like doing. Then the conversation she wanted to avoid had walked through her door anyway. "I guess."

"You guess? That doesn't sound good."

She shook her head. "No, that's not what I meant. I just found myself wondering what *all right* is. I mean... I've been coming home to this house for eight years, every night. I make myself a dinner, something usually better than this. Friends drop by. Sometimes I cook for all of us or go over to their places. But tonight nothing feels the same. I'm not sure anything is all right anymore."

He nodded slowly. "Life does things like that. Without warning, everything's off-center. It's like you have to reinvent yourself."

"That's a good description." She looked at him, taking in his attractive features. A little flutter reminded her she was a woman. "Tonight I feel like a stranger to myself."

"I know that feeling. That's why I stopped by. I could tell earlier you were having as much trouble with having *had* the vision as you were with what was in it."

She nodded, leaning back. "I sure wouldn't tell anyone else about it."

"That's what I wanted to suggest. Keep it quiet."

She didn't know if she liked that. Frowning, she asked, "Why? Because everyone will think I'm crazy? Because *you* think I'm crazy?"

He shook his head quickly, leaning forward. "I don't think you're crazy at all. Which is not to say I believe in psychics, but I've got an open mind and you obviously picked up on something. But you're certainly not crazy."

"Then why?"

"Because, if word gets around, it might put you in jeopardy with the killers."

Gut-punched. She couldn't even breathe. Stunned, she tried to absorb his words. Wings of panic started fluttering around the dark edges of her mind. Finally she said, "But I didn't identify anyone! I couldn't!"

"Do they know that?"

That was the question, wasn't it? "Are you trying to scare me?"

"I'm trying to protect you."

She couldn't doubt his sincerity. She'd heard that he'd been with the Department of Criminal Investigation before coming here to ranch. Gage apparently trusted him enough to ask for his help in the murder case. But even without that, something in his gaze seemed to reach out reassuringly. "I wasn't planning to tell anyone. Not even my friends. I keep these things to myself when they happen. Although it's usually nothing like this. Usually it's just a quick glimpse of something right before it happens."

He nodded and appeared to relax.

"I only told Emma because I couldn't hold it in anymore, and I trust her. She never gossips. Ever. But I couldn't bring myself to come in alone and tell Gage."

"Yet you felt you should."

She nodded. "It was like a pressure. Like something was pushing me, and it wouldn't leave me alone. Almost like someone was right at my shoulder, refusing to go away until I told you." She shuddered even now at the memory of that psychic push.

That caught his attention. "I take it you believe in the afterlife?"

Where did that come from? she wondered. "Most people do."

"I'm more of an agnostic. I don't know. But...you experienced it?"

She hesitated. Unlike some people, she didn't tell the story often, but rather hugged it to herself. "I don't know," she said honestly. "How could I? It's called a near-death experience, or NDE for short, because those of us who have it come back. The debate is about whether we experienced death at all, or just oxygen deprivation. There are widely separated camps on this."

"I would imagine so. But you must have made your own decision."

She bit her lower lip, searching his face, deciding she saw only genuine interest there. "Whatever I experienced, I have no doubt it was real, maybe more real than this chair I'm sitting in right now. I have no doubt that I had a glimpse of something so beautiful that there's no way I could describe it to you. It changed me. It certainly rid me of any fear of death."

He nodded, absorbing what she said, not immediately leaping forward with questions or conversation. She liked his thoughtful manner. She liked that he gave things time to settle as he took them in.

"I'm not so sure that's a good thing," he said presently.

"What?"

"Not being afraid of death."

At that she couldn't repress a smile. "I'm not jumping from airplanes without a parachute, if that's what you mean. I take reasonable precautions like everyone else. I'm just not afraid of the inevitable outcome of *every* life."

A smile creased his face in return. "Good point."

"We all get there sooner or later. The problem comes when we spend too much of our time and efforts trying to avoid it. I pity people who are obsessively afraid of dying."

"Anything can take over your life," he agreed. "That's a common obsession. Others of us have different ones."

She nodded, wondering if he was taking this conversation somewhere. At the same time, she didn't want him to leave. Earlier the house had felt empty and oppressive. Now it felt as home should. Normal sounds, warmth, friendliness. And she was feeling a kind of attraction she hadn't felt in quite a while. Was he married?

"Let me get you a coffee," she said. "And a slice of cheesecake. I imagine you spent most of the day outside." She paused, filled with the need to know. "Unless you need to get home to your family?"

This time he didn't decline. "No family," he said. "And coffee sounds really good now. It's getting cold out there."

So no family. That pleased her more than it probably should have. As she rose from the rocker, she took her congealing dinner tray to the kitchen, deciding she might as well have some cheesecake, too. Sometimes she needed comfort food, and tonight was a good night for it.

The wind blew some dead leaves against the kitchen window, rattling them as they passed. She stared out into the darkness, but saw only her own reflection in the glass. A lingering whiff of burned bacon wafted past her nose, barely detectable, and soon disappeared in the aromas of fresh coffee and chocolate-caramel cheesecake.

She placed everything on a serving tray, and returned to the living room, setting it down on the coffee table.

"Wow," he said appreciatively as he eyed the cheesecake. "Did you make this?"

"I get cravings for things like this sometimes. Besides, it's always good to have something like this on hand for visitors."

He smiled as she passed him a plate. "I need to drop by more often."

She laughed, inordinately pleased by the idea. "Just let me know if you mean that. I'll make sure not to run out of desserts."

He dug in with relish and complimented her generously. She sat back in her rocker, nibbling at her own slice, enjoying herself for the first time that day. The shadows that had haunted her had dispelled as if Adrian had brought light with him.

Life went on, she thought. Even when terrible things happened, people had to continue living. It was a hard-learned lesson, after her friends died in the accident. Sometimes she still felt guilty, very guilty, despite her experience of the light and her absolute conviction that her friends had gone to a far, far better place.

"Life has its charms," she said, before she realized she was going to speak out loud.

He looked at her with an arched brow. "It does," he agreed.

But she detected some kind of hesitancy in the way

he said it, a hesitation that convinced her he carried his share of ghosts, too. Maybe that's why he had gently steered her to talk about her near-death experience. Maybe he needed some kind of reassurance.

He rose suddenly, placing his plate and mug on the tray. "Can I carry this out to the kitchen for you?"

"No, no thanks. It's not a problem."

"It's time for me to be getting home," he said. "Tomorrow's going to be another long day."

"Yes." She nodded and stood, wondering why his mood had changed so abruptly.

He started toward the front door, then paused and looked back, his gray eyes serious. "Let us know if you sense anything else. Please."

The request surprised her, but what it hinted at made her shiver. "I hope I never sense another thing."

"I can sure understand why." He nodded, opened the door and disappeared into the dark evening as the door closed firmly behind him.

Kerry remained standing, ignoring an urge to get a sweater, thinking over his visit. It had been odd, she realized, about something other than what she had reported earlier.

But whatever had brought him, she was glad he had stopped by.

She heard the heat kick on, and as she carried the tray back to the kitchen, felt the first musty stirrings of hot air.

Time to put it all behind her, she decided. Today needed to be put on the shelf along with the other mysteries of her life, such as why she had survived an accident that had killed her two best friends.

Some questions just couldn't be answered.

Hours later, after a long, aimless drive, Adrian climbed out of his car in front of the small clapboard house he now called home. Around him spread the small ranch he had bought with his savings just before he retired with disability from the DCI.

The night, undisturbed by city lights, boasted a sky so strewn with stars that it looked like a black sea into which someone had tossed millions of diamonds. The swath of the Milky Way could be seen clearly, and its misty glow provided the answer to why the ancients had often believed it to be a heavenly river.

He loved it out here. The scent of sage and grass out-performed any aromatherapy. The minute he smelled the cool fragrant air, he always felt at peace.

He tried to soak up that feeling now, before entering his house, hoping to banish the day's images of mayhem. Trying to think of something pleasant.

Cheesecake. Yeah, that was pleasant. Good coffee, a cute schoolteacher...

But as soon as he tried to summon the images, reality called him back. Change that to unnerved and unnerving schoolteacher, pretty or not. For the first time he considered the possibility that being psychic could be real and, worse, it could be awful.

He'd had so-called psychics try to provide information before on his cases. On the rare occasions when they were right, no one knew until they'd developed the information through ordinary means anyway. As a result, he hadn't given the idea much thought over the years.

All that had changed in a few heart-stopping moments this evening when Kerry Tomlinson had described several unique aspects of the crime scene, aspects that couldn't have been known to her. Then she had said the bodies had been positioned to send a misleading message.

That statement drew him up short, because it was exactly what he had been thinking about the carefully posed bodies. Something he couldn't prove without a confession, something that on the face of it was a stretch.

Yet she had spoken his own impression aloud, an impression that he had shared only with Gage.

Impossible.

Except that when he looked up at the night sky, he sensed a universe that brimmed with possibilities that no one had yet imagined. Standing with his head tipped back, looking up at billions of suns, millions of which might have planets, hundreds of thousands of which might have life, he couldn't deny any possibility.

Certainly not after today.

Of course, he'd given up on the whole idea of anything being impossible when he'd discovered his own partner at DCI had turned on him. The last person on earth he would have ever expected to betray him. If that could happen, anything could.

Then, on the still night air, he heard two pops from far away. He froze, listening intently, wondering if they had been gunshots.

There could be so many reasons for someone to shoot at this time of night. This was ranch country. An injured or sick animal might need putting down. A coyote might have been preying on someone's sheep or chickens. So many legitimate reasons.

But something made him turn around and get back in his truck anyway.

Kerry turned in the damp sheets, eyes flittering to and fro beneath closed eyelids, her muscles rigid as if fighting to wake her....

"I'm starting to get really worried," Leah said to Georgia. "The guys should have joined us by now."

Georgia leaned closer to the campfire, seeking its warmth. "I didn't think it was going to get so cold so quickly."

"Georgia!"

Georgia looked up, smiling. "Cut it out, Leah. You're driving me crazy. The minute you put Hank and Bill into the woods, they turn into Lewis and Clark. We don't have to get back until Sunday, and neither of them is going to quit until they explore a cave or something. You know that."

Leah rubbed her jersey-clad arms. Her down vest ordinarily proved sufficient, but not tonight for some reason. "Something's wrong. I know it."

Georgia reached for a stick and poked at the fire, stirring up sparks, causing flames to leap higher. "Well, we can't leave the camp. They won't know where to look for us. So you're just going to have to relax until Sunday."

Leah finally quit pacing and came to sit on one of the dead logs they used as benches by the fire. "They always do this," she remarked.

"Exactly." Georgia smiled at her friend. "Every damn time. They say they'll be back by Friday so we can spend the weekend together, and they never make it. So relax. It just gives us more time for girl talk."

Leah managed a tight smile. "How many years have we been doing these trips?"

"Well, I know this is our eighth trip, and we always go twice a year so..." Georgia shook her head. "You know exactly how long we've been doing this. What are you trying to say?"

"I don't know."

Leah hunched toward the fire, wondering why she felt so on edge. This always happened. The guys went off by themselves to take some more rugged hikes while the girls stayed close to camp. The two men always returned late, usually because they'd found something exciting—it invariably surprised Leah what could excite a geologist—and when they marched into camp eventually, they always bubbled over about some find. Meanwhile Leah and Georgia were merely glad to enjoy the break from their jobs and spend a week in the woods with nothing to do but read good novels and relax.

Hugging herself, waiting for the warmth of the fire to penetrate, Leah looked up at the shadowy trees looming over them. "I've always loved the woods at night," she remarked.

"It's primal," Georgia said. She had a tendency to explain everything in life in terms of archetypes, genes and human psychology. That one simply had feelings never contented her. There always had to be a *reason*.

Leah shook her head. "How about I just *like* it?"

"But don't you want to understand yourself?"

"Not to the point that I atomize and pigeonhole everything."

This was an old disagreement, so old that it had become comfortable, and hence provided a good distraction.

Georgia sighed, a sound almost lost in the crackle of the fire. "You have no spirit of adventure."

"Adventure? Analyzing my every thought against some template is an adventure?"

Georgia grinned. "Then what do you think is an adventure?"

"Sitting in the woods at night around a campfire, listening to an owl hoot, and wondering where the hell the guys have gone."

"You *are* single-minded."

"No, just realistic." A twig snapped behind her in the woods and she looked around. "Did you hear that?"

"Yeah. Probably a raccoon."

"Or a wolf."

"Don't tell me you're afraid of wolves. Believe me, they're more scared of us."

"Then bears."

By this point both women were grinning at each

other, building a story from the crack of a branch. "Yeah, bears," Georgia agreed. "A mother and two cubs. Hungry. Annoyed because we're between them and the bacon grease I dumped up the hill this morning...."

"Ooooh," said Leah appreciatively, "that's it."

"Yeah. Are we supposed to run uphill or downhill?"

"I can't remember."

"Some adventurer you are..."

Just then a doe poked her head into the circle of light cast by the fire. Her eyes reflected red at them, and she froze.

"How beautiful," Georgia whispered.

"You're feeling a purely instinctual prey urge," Leah started to tease her in a whisper. "No appreciation of the beau—"

The word never fully left her mouth. Before her very eyes, Georgia's face transformed into a twisted mask as something sprayed from the side of her head. A split second later, a loud crack rent the night and echoed off the cliffside.

Leah froze like the deer had moments before, but the doe chose a different course, darting off into the woods.

Another crack and Leah felt a searing burn in her arm. She looked at it and saw a glistening wetness start to spread.

In the firelight, the wetness looked black.

Before she consciously comprehended what was happening, she turned away from the noise and fled into the night, running faster than she ever had in her life. Faster even than when she had been a sprinter in college.

Her body understood the situation even if her brain didn't...or wouldn't.

She had become the prey.

Kerry, who felt as if she had barely dropped off to sleep, woke up screaming from the nightmare. Even in her own ears the terrified sound seemed to echo. She sat up abruptly, feeling breathless, searching her room for a reason, a cause for the horrifying dream. Everything looked as it always did.

Just a dream, she told herself.

But then she switched on a light, climbed out of bed and began to dress. The compulsion could not be ignored.

Chapter 3

There were a lot of ways to make a living, Gage Dalton thought, that didn't involve climbing out of a warm bed in the wee hours, leaving behind the soft heat of a beautiful wife. His mouth twisted with grim humor at the thought, because all his adult life, with a break for recovery after a car bomb that had killed his first wife and family, he'd been doing exactly this. DEA, Conard County Sheriff's Office, all the same, just a difference in degrees.

The call from Kerry Tomlinson had sounded nearly panicky, and she insisted there was no time to waste. He was halfway down the stairs, headed for the front door when his cell rang. This time it was Adrian Goddard.

"I heard two gunshots," Adrian said. "I wish I could tell you for certain where they came from, but it *seemed* like the same general direction of the vics we found yesterday."

"I'm on my way to the office. Kerry just called me. Something's wrong but she could hardly talk and she said she had to get out of her house."

"I'm already on my way. Another ten minutes."

"See you there."

On impulse, as Gage clipped the phone to his belt, he turned around and headed back upstairs. He went to their son's room, the little boy they had agreed to adopt a couple of years ago. The three-year-old Jeremy at once filled Gage with blazing love and desperate terror. He knew what it was to lose a child. Bringing Jeremy into his life had been an act of faith more difficult than anything he'd ever done.

Peeking in, he saw that the restless child, as usual, dangled one leg over the edge of the bed, and barely had any covers over him at all. Moonlight, thin and weak, barely touched him.

Again on impulse, Gage scooped the sleeping child up. The boy barely stirred. He carried him in to the master bedroom and slipped him under the blankets with Emma.

Emma stirred, murmuring quietly, and with a mother's native instinct rolled over until she was wrapped around their child.

Gage adjusted the blankets a bit, then left as quietly as he could, sending up a prayer for their protection.

He thought he knew evil. He'd sure as hell seen enough horror. But tonight, somehow, he felt there was something even darker stalking this county.

* * *

Kerry waited, shaking, in her locked car outside the sheriff's office. What was taking Gage so damn long? She drummed her fingers nervously on the steering wheel, while the back of her neck prickled as if a predator watched her. No amount of telling herself it was just a dream could erase the urgency she felt. The terror she felt.

And this time she didn't care if anyone thought she was nuts.

At last headlights appeared, slicing through the darkness of the quiet main street. The moon, a mere sliver tonight, shed only the palest light, and the street lights, recently changed to stylish Victorian imitations, didn't seem to do much better. It was as if the darkness refused to give ground.

But at last the sheriff's SUV pulled into the reserved slot and she saw Gage's silhouette at the wheel. He climbed out quickly, after turning off his ignition, and came around to Kerry. She rolled her window down as he bent to look in.

"I think it'd be warmer inside, and I can make us some coffee or tea."

Clenching her teeth so they wouldn't chatter, she nodded, turned her own car off, and purse in hand followed him into the office.

The lighting was dim. The night dispatcher, a young deputy, half dozed at the console. He jumped when Gage and Kerry entered, but Gage waved him to relax. "Nothing?" he asked.

"Not a peep, just the regular check-ins."

"Start the coffee, would you? I think we're going to have a busy night."

At that the young deputy perked up. "I just made a pot. What's going on?"

"I'll know more after Adrian gets here. Just bring us the coffee, please. I need to get Kerry warmed up."

"Yeah, sure, Chief."

In his office, Gage turned on a portable electric heater to add its warmth to the air blowing through the vents in the floor. "Never gets warm enough back here," he remarked. "For myself I don't mind. That's what jackets and sweaters are for, but you look like you need to thaw out."

Kerry nodded gratefully. "I don't think I've ever felt this cold. Ever. And it's not that cold outside."

"Adrian's on his way," he said again as the young deputy entered and brought them coffee. Kerry suddenly remembered she'd had him in English class only two or three years ago. Calvin Henry, that was his name. "Thanks, Cal," she said.

He smiled. "Anytime, Ms. Tommy." The name the students called her. He looked at Gage. "Anything else?"

"Just send Adrian back here. I'll let you know when I know."

Cal nodded and walked out.

"Why is Adrian coming?"

Gage hesitated.

"Gage, please." She needed something, anything, to right her reeling world.

"He heard a couple of gun shots tonight. From the same general direction where we found our vics."

That was not what she needed. Not to set her world right. All it did was cause her to teeter more.

"Two women," she said. "One is dead. The other wounded and running." Her voice rose, almost to a keen. "Oh, God, Gage. We have to get out there! She's running and alone!"

The convoy built as Gage led the way out toward the place where the murders had happened. Deputies and state police pulled off their routes and out of bed created a steadily lengthening train behind him. Kerry, in the backseat, leaned forward and looked between Gage and Adrian toward the dark hulk of the mountains ahead of them.

"Keep watching to the right," she said suddenly. "The women had a campfire. You might catch a glimpse of it."

"How far right?" Adrian asked.

Kerry closed her eyes. "One or two o'clock," she said finally. "I'm not a hundred percent certain, but that's what I keep seeing."

"You got it."

"Tell me about the dream again," Gage said quietly.

"I already did."

"I might pick out an important detail that I missed before."

"All right." Cold to the bone, despite the blast from the car's heater, she forced herself to summon the images that had scared her awake.

"Two women," she said. "Friends. They camp a lot together. They were waiting for someone who was delayed."

"Any idea who?"

Kerry started to shake her head then. "My God! I think they were waiting for the men who were killed. One of them was worried, but the other wasn't. As if...as if these guys are often late getting back to camp."

Gage looked at Adrian. "That's a link we didn't have before."

Adrian nodded. "Anything else, Kerry?"

"Just the same thing as before. I saw the side of a woman's head explode. Then the other one was hit in the arm. She started running, away from the shots. She's cold and terrified, and I think...I think she's hiding. I think she found a place to hide."

"Is she still being hunted?"

Kerry squeezed her eyes shut, reaching even though she didn't want to, trying to pull more substance out of the nightmare that had torn her from sleep. "I don't know. I just don't know."

Gage pressed on the accelerator. "Then we'd better move even faster."

Radios crackled back and forth throughout the trip, ideas shared, plans for the search worked out. No one seemed very hopeful they could find anything before dawn. The night was too dark, and once they got into the woods, it would only become impenetrable.

But dawn was no longer far away.

* * *

Ten minutes later, just as it seemed they were about to enter the abyssal darkness of the woods, Adrian leaned forward in his seat. Then he spoke above the radio chatter. "I think I see a campfire. About two o'clock. I can only catch it out of my peripheral vision, though."

Kerry understood. Once you began operating on night vision, the clearest images were peripheral. She'd first noticed that when studying the sky at night as a girl. Some stars were so faint that you could only see them when you looked far enough to the side.

"There's a fence road up just ahead," Gage replied. "I'll take a right turn on it. Tell the rest of the crew."

The message passed by radio. Two minutes later Gage turned them onto a track that clearly served no other purpose than to allow a pickup to ride along a ranch fence.

"Chester McNair's place," Gage said, as if giving a travelogue.

"That's where the others were found."

"I know. I know. But you've seen Chester and his kids. The only way they could be involved in this is because they let hikers traverse the ranch where it abuts the state forest."

"Why does he do that anyway?"

"Because above that point the terrain gets really difficult to cross. Besides, Chester thinks it helps keep the wolves away from his place. He might be right. Those wolves are so damn shy it's hard to know how many of them we have up there."

Kerry spoke, trying to cling to normalcy even though her heart had begun to hammer. "I have a friend who works in the zoology department at the university. She says they just about despair of finding a number anywhere close to exact."

"They can range these mountains from Texas to Alaska, and beyond," Adrian agreed. "Good for them. We never should have hunted them in the first place."

Kerry decided this reserved ex-lawman could be likable as well as sexy. The thought shocked her, seeming as it did so out of place under the present circumstances. But there it was, as if her brain and body were trying to remind her that life was good, that life continued, that whatever lay up ahead, it didn't have to uproot her from her own reality.

A soft sigh escaped her, because she suddenly wished she could believe her life would ever be normal again.

"There it is," Adrian said, now pointing to the left. Somehow the road had turned them around.

Kerry looked, but wasn't certain she saw more than a dull orange glow up the mountainside a bit. Almost as soon as she looked at it, it vanished.

"I see," Gage said. He immediately pulled the SUV over beside the rusty fence and put on his flashers. Then he aimed his spotlight up toward the woods.

"Roof flashers," Adrian suggested. "In case the woman can see us. To reassure her."

Gage nodded and hit the switch. Instantly, swirling red and blue lights joined the spotlight glare. Behind them, more than a dozen other vehicles pulled to a stop and followed suit.

Gage turned on the seat and looked at the two of them. "I don't want to leave Kerry here alone, so you stay with her, Adrian."

"No," Kerry said, astonishing herself. "I have to come with you. Whatever's up there, I need to see it for myself." Because it would verify her vision? Or because she hoped to find out she was wrong and could stop worrying about visions altogether? She didn't know. "Besides, I may be able to help find the survivor."

Gage looked as if he'd swallowed cod liver oil, but after a couple of beats nodded. "Okay. Just stick close to the two of us, no matter what."

"I'm not crazy. But I have to see."

And she didn't feel as if she could fight what was happening any longer, not if a woman was out there hiding, wounded and terrified.

She'd left her house dressed warmly, and wearing jeans and hiking boots, as if at some level she'd known this would come. At this point she couldn't have said for certain whether her clothing choices had merely been practical in response to feeling cold, or whether something else had guided her.

For better or worse, something had taken over her life. She just hoped it was temporary because right now she felt as if she blindly climbed onto a roller coaster and now all she could do was endure the ride to the finish.

They used the bullhorns first, the amplifiers on the cars, announcing they were police, and they were coming into the woods. Some objected on the grounds that they might scare off the killer. Gage remained firm.

"We have reason to believe there's a wounded woman hiding out there. At this point she's my top priority."

Kerry gave thanks that no one asked how Gage had come by his information. Of course, she realized, word of her vision might already be spreading. Cops gossiped like anyone else.

Regardless, after announcing repeatedly to the dark woods that they were cops, they picked up flashlights and shotguns, spread out and began to climb in a carefully spaced line toward the dull glow of the dying campfire.

With their arrival, the forest had silenced itself, except for one annoyed owl that complained from a treetop up the slope. The distance to the fire's glow didn't seem that great, but the climb was taxing and slowed them down considerably. Not far in space, Kerry thought as her nerves stretched tighter and tighter, but endless in time. The owl continued to comment from the sidelines.

"We probably scared all the little critters into their holes," Adrian remarked to Kerry. "His dinner vanished."

"Most likely." She leaned forward and grabbed a rock for support as the ground turned even steeper for a short distance. The darkness thickened around them, and the flashlights seemed less and less able to penetrate it. Her sense of foreboding deepened with every step. Her heart, already accelerating with exertion, began to hammer.

The law officers, men and women, periodically called to one another, keeping themselves together when a flashlight would suddenly disappear from view behind a boulder or in a gully. They only quieted when they paused to listen for human sounds. A cry for help maybe. And sometimes, as if it appreciated what they were doing, the irritated owl fell silent with them.

But no human voice called out to them. The woods, fragrant with pine and spruce, might have been empty except for them and the owl.

Kerry's reluctance grew. The urge to turn and flee kept rising from the pit of her stomach even as something seemed to keep pulling her forward. She didn't want to be part of this. She wanted to be somewhere else, tucked safely away in sleep, unaware that such ugliness and horror shared the planet with her. Vain wish, she knew, but reading it in the papers was a far cry from this. Dread marched beside her in a way it never had before.

Finally the glow of the campfire came into clearer view. Steps quickened, and from along the whole line of searchers, people gasped for air as they hurried up the steep slope, Kerry among them. Each and every one of them was propelled by the hope of arriving in time to save a life. Any other thought faded into inconsequence.

At the last second, though, Adrian grabbed Kerry and turned her away from the fire, pressing her face into the shoulder of his nylon parka. "You don't want to see," he said.

A part of her wanted to agree with him, but that pressure inside her head was back, demanding, calling, urging. She could no more resist than she could have vanished from the spot.

She pulled her head back, reluctantly stepping out of the protective circle created by his arms. "I've already seen," she said unsteadily.

"Not in real life," he argued gently.

"I think I have."

Turning, she faced the glowing campfire and stepped forward. She sucked a shocked breath.

Not because of the scene, but because she had already seen it so accurately. It was *real*.

The world darkened, leaving only a pinpoint of light, then even that turned black.

Chapter 4

Adrian caught Kerry just as she started to topple. Holding her beneath her arms, he moved her away from the ugly crime scene, just a few feet, just enough to conceal it from her. Then he gently lowered her to the ground, sat with his back propped against a tree, and cradled her head on his lap. The warmth generated by the climb deserted him almost immediately. For the first time he realized just how cold it had become, but the fact barely registered in his concern for Kerry.

She returned to consciousness almost as soon as she reached horizontal.

"What happened?" she asked.

"You fainted."

"I don't faint."

"You just did, sorry to say." He couldn't stop himself from reaching out to stroke her hair soothingly, and was surprised by how silky it felt. Nor could he swallow the concern he was beginning to feel for her. "It's been a rough twenty-four hours," he continued. "I'm not surprised you couldn't take any more. And that was a shock."

"But I'd seen it in my dream. It looked exactly like my dream." A shiver passed through her. "I think that's what's so horrible. It was *exactly* like my dream."

That comment truly gave him pause. Ugly as the murder scene was, he had to admit it would be equally, if not more, shocking to realize you had seen it precisely in a dream. Unfamiliar uneasiness tickled the base of his skull as it struck him that he hadn't fully believed her before. That part of him had held back, not wanting to accept that she really *did* represent something beyond his ken.

Shivering again, she turned toward him and pressed her face against his hip. A sizzle of unwanted excitement passed through him, then submitted to his will. No room for that right now. He patted her shoulder, then rubbed it gently.

"The ground is cold," he said, conflicted by desires to protect and to get some distance. "You shouldn't lie on it longer than necessary."

She nodded. He felt the motion through the denim as he continued to rub her shoulder.

Already the crime scene tape was being strung, and they were within the circle. Flashlights were scouring the ground for evidence of any kind.

Kerry groaned and sat up. Adrian kept a steadying hand against her back. "I'm not done," she said. "There's more here...somewhere."

"What?"

She didn't answer, but struggled to regain her feet. He arose behind her, moving quickly, ready to catch her if she fainted again. But it was as if some kind of steel had stiffened her.

She walked toward the campfire. Gage stepped toward her, as if to stop her, but then halted. Everyone halted, watching Kerry. It was as if they knew something was about to happen.

She tilted her head back, eyes closed, avoiding the now-covered body on the ground. Then her arm lifted slowly and she pointed. "She's out that way. Hiding. She's weak. You have to hurry."

Perhaps even stranger than Kerry's announcement, Adrian thought, was the way not a soul questioned her. Gage gave the order and the searchers fanned out again in the direction she indicated. Gage went with them, after ordering Adrian, Kerry and two officers to remain at the scene.

The wind shifted without warning, probably driven by the warmth of approaching dawn, and the stench of death overcame the smell of the pines. Adrian drew Kerry away, to where the breeze freshened with life.

"Are you okay?" Adrian asked her.

"Yeah." She nodded slightly. "It's starting to let go."

"What do you mean?"

"The compulsion." She lifted her gaze to his. "I don't

know what's worse, the fact that I'm having these visions or the fact that I feel so compelled to act on them. It's like being pressed from behind and not allowed to gain your footing, if you know what I mean."

"Like being pushed by a crowd?"

"It feels something like that." She shook her head and wrapped her arms around herself. "I can't ignore it. And I'll be honest with you, if it saves that woman's life, it's worth it." But she would still have to live with it, and the idea soured her mouth.

"It certainly would be."

"I just hope this never happens again."

He put an arm around her shoulders, telling himself he wanted to help warm her, but in all honesty he couldn't have said which of them he wanted to warm. He had put his judgment about what was happening with Kerry on hold until later, when he could review in retrospect, but it remained he wasn't sure what was happening here, and if they found a wounded woman tonight, he knew he was going to dislike what he would have to believe.

Kerry leaned into him, still holding herself, seeming grateful for the support. The calls of the search team were steadily moving away, upslope. Adrian looked up at the sky, and thought he saw a faint grayness outlining the tops of the dark trees. Soon daylight would answer other questions.

All of a sudden he felt Kerry stiffen.

"What's wrong?" he asked.

She whispered, "He's out there. Watching."

Adrian lowered his voice. "Who's out there?"

"The killer."

Adrian felt the back of his neck prickle. "Where?"

She moved closer. "I'm not sure. I just feel him. He won't shoot now."

"How many?"

She shook her head. "I think only one, but it feels like someone else could be involved, too."

"Hell." He muttered the word and turned her so that she had a tree at her back and him at her front. "Remind me to get you a vest."

"Vest?"

"Armor."

The relative quiet of the scene began to give way to the sounds of people coming up the slope from below. Flashlights appeared, their beams darting around.

"The coroner and the crime scene unit," Adrian said. They came from a neighboring, more heavily populated county. "That was fast. Where do I tell them to start looking for the killer?"

"Don't tell them, Adrian." She shook her head. "Look, it was just a funny feeling. Whatever. I don't even know if he's watching. It came and went in an instant. I don't want to be the county freak show."

"I understand," he said. "So I'll have them secure the scene here. But you'll have to stay with them, and I mean right beside them, because no matter what you say, I have to go out and look for tracks, if there are any. So what direction do I look?"

Kerry tried to lock in on the feeling again, but it was

gone for good. She pointed vaguely. "That way, I think. But I can't be sure."

"Okay. You stay with the coroner till I get back."

Another shudder passed through Kerry as she nodded. "You know, you don't have to protect me. There are other cops around."

"Let me, it's good for my ego." Few things were anymore.

At that, even in the very dim light, he saw her smile.

"It's an awful night," she said.

"Among the worst."

"I don't want these visions and dreams anymore."

"I don't blame you."

"It's awful knowing something and being unable to stop it. Like standing in front of a train."

"I can only imagine." Which wasn't completely true. He'd had a glimpse of that particular nightmare, but only a glimpse, and it still haunted his life.

"But if we get that woman," she repeated without finishing the statement, more to herself than him. As if to remind herself once again that some good might come out of this.

"I guess that would go some way to making this experience a little easier to live with." If anything could. Old bitterness tasted like bile in his throat, but the last thing he wanted to tell her was that some things never grew easier. Ever.

She nodded again, then turned her head to watch the crime scene people arrive and scatter around. A portable generator roared to life. It wasn't long before flood lights and photo flashes punctured the night, and markers began to cover the ground.

Kerry waited with the coroner while Adrian briefly circled through the woods. He returned ten minutes later, shaking his head. He found her sitting against a rock, her face illuminated from the side by all the lights. When she said "Hello," her voice was almost lost in the roar of the portable generator. He couldn't connect with whatever she was feeling, except that it must be like the hunches that had once guided him. He decided that for now he had to trust her as he had always trusted his hunches. There didn't seem to be another choice.

"We'll search the perimeter again when we've got decent light," he said by way of reassurance. "But that guy isn't out there now."

"I know. There're too many people around now," she answered. She leaned her head back against the tree, and closed her eyes. "I don't know how I'm going to teach today."

"You're not. Call in sick. Tell 'em you're helping the cops. Whatever. But you're not going to work."

Her eyes snapped open, weary and red. "Why not? It's not your decision."

"Well, let me put it this way. You said the killers were watching."

"So?"

"So they know you were here. And maybe they know you're not a cop. Maybe these bastards know exactly who you are. No, Kerry, whether you go to work today or not, you're going to be under protection from here on out."

Her eyes widened, whether at the determination in his voice or his choice of epithet, but before she could respond there was a shout from up the mountain. They both tensed, listening, then another shout reached them.

"She's alive!"

The ambulance pulled away with the victim while the sky lightened to a pale blue. Color returned to the world, reminding Kerry that it could still be a beautiful place. The night's horrors seemed to be washed away.

"She's conscious," Gage told her and Adrian as he approached his car where they waited. "Suffering from exposure and blood loss, and pretty dazed, but still conscious."

"Thank God!" Kerry said. For an instant she actually felt blessed to have had that nightmare. But almost as soon as she felt that, she crashed again. She was exhausted, her hands had gotten scraped up during the climb, and all she wanted was for life to return to normal. As if it ever could.

Without another word, she climbed into the backseat of Gage's vehicle and closed her eyes. Fatigue instantly carried her to the borderland between sleep and waking, and distantly she felt the car start and begin to bump down the road. She could hear Gage and Adrian talking, but their voices were quiet and she had no energy to strain to hear them. Even ten minutes ago she would have believed she was too keyed up to sleep for hours, but as soon as the car hit the smoother surface of the county road, her head lolled back and she fell into a deep, dreamless place.

Escape. For a little while. She had absolutely no idea that the discussion in the front seat indirectly involved her.

"I can't do it," Adrian said. "And you know why."

"It's not the same situation," Gage replied. "Look, she's not a criminal informant like the one you worked with before. Giving her protection is a just a precaution, not a necessity."

"I can't do it. You know what happened. I don't trust myself."

"Why? Because your partner lied to you and killed your informant? That's a whole different kettle of fish."

"No, because I can't trust *myself.*"

Gage fell silent for a moment, then said, "Then it's time you learned how to again."

A car door slammed, waking her, then she heard Gage say, "I'll bring it over."

Wanting to groan, she opened her eyes to a bright autumn morning, just as Adrian opened the car door for her. Blinking, she stared at him, trying to place herself in time and space.

"We're at your house," Adrian said. "Gage is going to have someone bring your car back from the police station. Keys?"

Automatically her hand went to her jacket pocket and she pulled them out. "House key," she said, surprised by how dry her mouth felt.

"I'll unlock the door," Adrian reassured her. "The car keys are on this ring as well?"

"Yes."

As Adrian walked away, she rubbed her eyes and yawned.

"I'll call the school," Gage said. "They won't expect you before Monday at the earliest."

"Thanks." At this point she was past wondering what excuse he'd give, and what kind of gossip would begin to make the rounds. Not that it mattered. Gossip pulsed through the arteries of this community like blood, most of it simply newsy, not malicious. Right now all she cared about was a tall glass of water and her bed.

"There we go." Adrian's voice reached her as he came round the car to the driver's side and handed Gage the keys through the window.

"I know you'll take care of her," Gage said. There seemed to be some kind of undercurrent in his tone.

Take care of her? The words galvanized Kerry enough to slide off the seat and out of the car. Her legs felt stiff as she turned and faced her house. The door beckoned her, and beyond it the bed.

She probably should have said something to Gage, but the car door slammed and he drove away almost before the thought formed and reached awareness. Adrian's hand gripped her elbow gently.

"To bed with you," he said kindly.

"Water first."

"Water first," he agreed.

Inside everything looked normal, which for some reason surprised her. She filled a glass at the tap of the kitchen sink and downed it in one long draft before re-filling it and drinking again. God, she was thirsty!

"Thanks," she said to Adrian as she walked past him toward the hallway and her bedroom at the back of the house. "Please lock the door when you leave?"

"Sure," he said.

She couldn't imagine why he sounded so amused, nor at that moment did she care. She fell facedown on her bed without even removing her boots. Tension, it seemed, had taken an even greater toll than a nearly sleepless night.

She awoke during the early afternoon feeling cruddy, filthy and sore all over. Where ordinarily she might have taken a few minutes to savor waking up, she couldn't wait to push herself out of bed, strip off her dirty clothes and boots and climb into the shower. Under the hot, stinging spray, muscles began to ease and her mind began to work.

She was sorry when it did. Last night insisted on popping to the forefront of her thoughts, and she realized reluctantly that she needed to run it over and over until she could assimilate it. That was what she had needed to do after the accident, and the hospital psychologist had told her that was a perfectly normal coping mechanism. Only when it was interrupted did problems arise.

So she shouldn't interrupt it, but she'd like to put it off until after she'd eaten something.

Finally, dressed in fresh jeans and a baggy flannel shirt, with her hair wrapped in a towel, she emerged from her bedroom with one goal in mind: the kitchen.

She stopped in astonishment on the threshold as she encountered Adrian. He was still here. What was more, he was cooking bacon, from the aroma, and had a bowl of beaten eggs beside the stove.

And coffee. Oh, Lord, she needed the coffee.

"Take a seat," he said as if he invited her to her own table every day. "Coffee black, right?"

"Right."

He turned from the stove to grab a cup from the cupboard, and filled it with dark, steaming brew. Then he put it on the table. How did he know where she usually sat?

Somehow he did, and she rounded the table to take her seat.

"I heard you get in the shower," he said. "I figured you must be hungry."

"Starved." She reached for the mug and took a cautious sip. "Mmm, you make good coffee."

"Thanks. How crispy do you like your bacon?"

"Just a little."

"Rye toast?"

"Please."

Sip after sip, the caffeine reached her brain and with it a sense that right now everything was okay. It might not stay that way, but for now she enjoyed the illusion.

She looked at his back. "Heard any more about the survivor?"

"She's going to make it. And she didn't see anything at all except her friend getting shot. She said they were waiting for their husbands to come back from an extended hike. Apparently the men were geologists as well as hikers."

"Does she know yet...about...?" She couldn't bring herself to finish the question.

"Not sure yet," he said, turning with the frying pan to fork strips of bacon onto a plate covered with a paper towel. "She's not too coherent yet, and remember, we found no ID on the male vics. Can't be absolutely certain."

She shook her head sadly. "Those were their husbands, you know."

"Likely, yeah."

"That poor woman."

"I've got a suggestion," he said as he drained the grease from the pan.

"Yes?"

"Let's think about something else. I found over the years that it's easy to let these things take over your life. You certainly don't need to do that."

"No, you're right," she agreed. "But it's like something I can't shake."

He set the pan back on the stove and turned the flame to low. "Let's work on it. Normalcy must be maintained."

Something about the way he said it made her chuckle, a reluctant sound. Some part of her whispered that she ought to be crying, not laughing and living, and getting ready to eat. "Believe me, I'd be happy to have *every-thing* return to normal. Somehow I don't think it will."

"Eventually it'll feel normal again." He spoke with the certainty of experience, she thought, and took comfort from it. "There's a difference between normal and the same."

"You've got a point."

"Of course!" He flashed an attractive smile and poured the beaten eggs into the pan.

Kerry looked down into her coffee mug, trying to center herself in the here and now. Adrian's presence aided her because she wasn't at all used to having anyone else cook in her kitchen, and most certainly not a man. A good-looking man. A nice man. That's what she needed to focus on, not nightmares and visions.

Besides, she told herself stoutly, she was probably done with that whole mess now, and could resume her usual life. Whatever had connected her to those events was gone now, surely, especially since her connection had seemed to be with the victims, not the killers. Experience had long ago taught her that you couldn't just stop living because something awful had happened.

They ate together at the table. Adrian proved to be a master with eggs, perfectly cooked without a hint of brown to embitter them. The bacon was just right, too, chewy with just a hint of crunch.

"Do you enjoy teaching?" he asked her as he passed her the stack of toast.

"Nothing else could make me do it."

His eyes twinkled. "That bad?"

"No, it's not. I love it. It's just that it requires a lot of patience, a lot of planning, a lot of people skills and the pay isn't that great. If you don't love it, you won't last long. But I guess you can say that about a lot of jobs."

"I imagine so. People certainly don't go into teaching to get wealthy."

"Or ranching."

He chuckled. "Not these days. Like you said, a lot of hard work and the pay is lousy. Not that I'm deeply into it yet."

"What drew you to it?"

"Having a piece of wide-open space for myself."

That struck a chord with her. "That would be so nice."

"It is."

"Is someone taking care of your livestock?"

He tilted his head a little. "I have a hired hand, but I don't have a lot of livestock. I'm not sure how far down that road I want to go. I grew up on a ranch so I wouldn't be a complete tyro, but on the other hand, I left the ranch. Coming back doesn't necessarily mean I want to get involved in the business side. Right now I have a few saddle horses, and some mustangs I adopted and let range free. Beyond that, I haven't made any decisions."

"Sounds nice," she admitted. "A bit of freedom."

"For now. Like everyone else, though, I'll have to figure it all out sooner or later. A man needs to work at something."

"Why'd you leave the department?" As soon as she asked the question, she knew she'd gotten too personal. The man who had seemed relaxed just the instant before, stiffened.

He put his fork down, frowning in a way that deepened the lines on his face. "Some...bad stuff happened," he said finally. "I'm out on disability."

He wasn't telling her something, of that she was sure, but she didn't press any further on it. Hard to believe they had met for the first time only yesterday. Events had conspired to make her feel closer to him than she really was. She needed to keep that in mind.

They washed the dishes together then retired to the living room. The first thing Kerry noticed was the bullet-proof vest lying on an ottoman. "That's not for me," she said, denying it.

"Yes, it is. I had Gage send it over."

She shook her head. "No, I don't think so. I don't need it."

He touched her shoulder with his fingertips until she looked from the vest to him. "Think about it, Kerry. You said the killers were up there watching last night. If they figure out who you are, that you're not a cop, that you're the one feeding us information, do you really think you'll be safe?"

"There's no reason to think they know anything about my visions!"

He shook his head. "Get real. Do you really think *all* those cops are going to manage to keep their mouths shut? Even with the best intentions, if one tells his wife and she tells a friend, it gets all over the county. Or if one tells her husband."

"Adrian!"

"No, think about it. One loose mouth and that's it. And husbands and wives tend to trust each other with stuff even when it's supposed to be confidential. Or one guy trusts a friend. You were up there with us last night.

You pointed out the direction the woman had fled. Everyone was listening to you. Some of the guys may not know why we were listening to you. They may think you're an informant. Either way, if the killers identify you, they'll know you know something about them. And these guys clearly don't care who they shoot."

She didn't want to accept his argument, but with a sinking sensation she knew he was right. If these killers thought anyone might be able to finger them for any reason, that person might well wind up in their crosshairs. Adrian certainly believed so.

And for some reason, she trusted both him and his judgment. Right now, she wasn't sure she trusted her own at all. And while dying didn't frighten her anymore, she was hardly in a rush to do it again. Life still offered opportunities she wanted to enjoy, like eventually marrying and having children, or the look on a student's face when a connection finally happened. Lots of things worth living for.

She dropped gracelessly onto the sofa. "Okay," she said grimly. "Okay. But not in the house." Life may have put her on a roller coaster again, leaving her feeling exhausted and depressed, but her native stubbornness refused to cede every inch of her existence to the horror these killers were creating. If stubbornness was all she had to prop her up through this, then stubbornness it would be.

"And I'm going to stay here," he announced flatly. "You're not going to be alone again until these guys are caught."

At that her head jerked up. "What if I'm not comfortable having you around all the time? What if I like my privacy?"

"You gave that up when you came to us with these visions." There was a fire in his eyes now, a fire that warned her they were getting near to something that made him dangerous. Whatever it was, this wasn't the time. She could see that in every line of him. She smothered an uncharacteristic urge to swear at the impossible situation.

Finally she nodded. "So I'm a prisoner?"

"No. You're under protection."

She grabbed a throw pillow and hugged it. "Then why does it feel the same?"

"Only because you haven't been imprisoned. You can't imagine how bad it really is."

"Cold comfort."

"Yeah, probably." He sat down beside her. "But I can't let anything happen to you."

The word *can't* caught her attention. Maybe because she was an English teacher and very aware of the word's proper use. Or maybe, she thought, because she sensed he *had* used the word properly.

What was going on here? And how long was it going to last?

She might as well have been cast adrift on a stormy ocean, with no land in sight and no compass to guide her. Once again, as after the accident, she felt everything had flown out of her control.

She *hated* that feeling.

Chapter 5

Casino-quality poker chips clattered steadily as the two men sat beneath an overhead light. They liked to play with their chips, riffling them as they considered their next move. Across the table from them sat a woman, filling in as dealer. She was the younger man's wife, but the older man was in control of everything. She had no idea what they were playing for, nor did she care. When they played they weren't giving *her* a hard time.

She was glad to see the older man was heading toward a win. He hadn't been happy the other day when he lost.

A baby wailed from the next room, and she looked at her husband. He nodded his permission, so she jumped up and went to take care of their son.

The two men at the table exchanged looks.

"What was the schoolteacher doing there?" the older man asked the younger.

"I told you, I don't know. But they were all listening to her. I couldn't figure it out."

"You must have screwed something up." The older man stood, shoving his huge stack of chips to the side. "Did you talk to anyone?"

"Do you really think I'm that stupid?"

"See if Cal knows anything. He used to be your friend."

"He still is. I'll sound him out."

"But be careful." The older man pointed to the chips. "I get to choose this time. Make sure I don't choose you."

The younger man froze, then nodded. "Look, man, it's just a game. That's what you said."

"Yeah. Unless we get caught. You already messed it up by not getting both of them."

"She didn't see me. No way. Damn it, she was next to the fire and it was dark. She couldn't have seen anything even if I'd been close, but I was so far away that she wouldn't have been able to see me in broad daylight."

"That's what you say." The older man shook his head. "I told you, it's more exciting than stalking deer. But it's also more dangerous, 'cause these deer can talk. Remember that, and don't miss your next shot."

"I won't."

Finally the older man smiled and returned to the table. Picking up a stack of chips, he began to riffle them. "It's better than going all-in at Vegas, isn't it?"

The young guy grinned. "You bet."

"The ultimate gamble."

"The ultimate thrill."

The two men were still laughing when the woman returned to the room with the child in her arms.

Adrian sat in the easy chair in Kerry's living room, reading a history of the Napoleonic Wars. The floor lamp over his shoulder cast the only light in the room. He'd drawn the insulated drapes over the sheers on Kerry's front windows, ensuring that no one could see into the room from outside.

Kerry herself, apparently able to relax for the first time since all this had begun, had fallen asleep again, this time on the couch. A crocheted afghan covered her, and a paperback book still dangled from one hand. He had thought about removing it, but was afraid he would wake her.

Instead he sat watching her, thinking what a beautiful woman she was. She had the quiet kind of beauty that he had always liked. He also wondered why the hell he'd allowed himself to be pressured into protecting her. He should have learned his lesson on that one. He had no business accepting this kind of trust.

Yet, oddly, he didn't trust anyone else to do it. Or maybe not so oddly, given what had happened with his partner.

At times, the urge to walk out of here before he garnered another nightmare nearly overwhelmed him. Twice he considered calling Gage and telling him to put a deputy on this.

But he couldn't do it. He couldn't turn this woman over to anyone else's protection. If he did that and something went wrong, it would be the nightmare all over again anyway. Any way he looked at it, it was a lose-lose situation unless he brought Kerry safely through this.

But he hardly felt adequate.

Rising, he walked through her small house, once again checking doors and windows, making sure that every possible curtain was drawn. Even with the heavy curtains in most of the rooms, the night's chill crept in through invisible crannies in the old house, stirring up icy drafts. He expected there'd be frost by morning. The first frost.

Just as he was about to walk out of the kitchen, the phone rang. He leaped for the wall set, hoping to catch it before it woke Kerry.

He grabbed it just as the second ring began. He expected to hear Gage's voice.

"Hello?"

Silence. Then a *click,* followed by the drone of an empty line.

He returned the phone to its cradle, frowning. Wrong number? Or something else? His hand hovered over the receiver, but after a moment he decided it wasn't enough to call Gage about. People dialed wrong numbers all the time, and an amazing number of them weren't even polite enough to say, "Sorry, wrong number." He tried *69, but received a message, "Number not available." Okay, then, probably an automated sales call. There sure were enough of those during any given evening.

As he returned to the living room, Kerry was sitting up. "Who was on the phone?"

"Wrong number," he answered with more certainty than he felt.

She nodded and hid a yawn behind her hand. "Sorry, I don't know why I'm so sleepy."

"No need to apologize." He settled into the easy chair. "You've had a stressful time. Stress takes it out of you faster than lack of sleep."

"I guess!" She rubbed her eyes gently with her fingertips. "You're going to go crazy sitting around here with nothing to do except watch me."

He picked up the book he'd been reading and showed it to her. "You have a pretty good selection for an English teacher."

At that she smiled, filling him with pleasure. "I'm a bit of a dilettante when it comes to books. My students may think I only read Shakespeare, Sophocles and Dickens, but the best thing I can say about living here is that we don't have a book store big enough for me to go broke in."

At that he laughed. "But you can order online."

"And I do. But it's harder to just browse there. When I go to the mall my bank account takes a nuclear hit."

"Have you read all those books in the next room?"

"Almost all."

"Wow. I love to read, too, but I've never had a library anything like yours."

She curled her legs beneath her, still smiling, and tugged the afghan around her shoulders. "I go beyond loving to read. I love the books themselves. The way they feel in my hands, the smell of them, the weight of them. I'll probably always be a Luddite when it comes to books. I can't imagine getting the same pleasure from reading an electronic version."

"The younger generation probably will."

"Maybe. But they still use books in classes."

He raised a teasing eyebrow. "And that's supposed to be a recommendation?"

She laughed. "You might have a point there. My sophomores are currently complaining about having to read *Antigone*. I should put it on as a play, so they'd get the impact as it was written, but I don't have the actors."

"Maybe you should appeal to the community. Or the local theater group. I know they usually only manage to produce a couple of plays a year, but maybe some of them would enjoy doing something like that."

She nodded. "That's a great idea. I'd hoped to get students to do it. I'd like to crack a few more nuts than I do now. Literature is important, of course, but reading and writing are equally so, and there are connections there that a lot of kids don't seem to get. It's as if they don't understand how fundamentally important communication is, apart from talking to each other. And texting! That's killing writing."

He gave a quiet chuckle. "Tell you what. Why don't we arrange to bring some of your classes out to my ranch? I've got some great rock paintings out there. Maybe it'll impress them that thousands of years ago the native peoples were leaving messages for each other."

She brightened at that. "I never thought about that."

"It's basically the same thing, in a different medium. Think how critical that kind of communication must have been for them, that they'd go to all the trouble to paint or carve symbols on rocks to pass something along."

She was nodding, clearly liking the idea. "Yeah. It all began with the need to pass information, and it kept growing."

"What's more, it's always been an art form."

Just then the phone rang. It was on the end table beside her, so before he could reach it, she had lifted the cradle to her ear.

"Hello?"

He watched her face drain white, and her hand start to shake. A second later she slammed the receiver down.

"What?" he demanded. "What was that?"

"A man." Her voice cracked. "He said I'm next."

Gage arrived twenty minutes later, accompanied by the former sheriff, Nate Tate. Nate's decision to retire didn't mean that anyone had stopped treating him as if he were still in the job he'd held for more than thirty years.

Nate himself looked hale, his permanently sunburned face lined with weather and the responsibilities he'd held for so long. But he also emitted a warmth that made most people trust and like him.

"So what the hell is going on?" Nate demanded as they all settled in the living room, Adrian on the sofa beside Kerry. "How would anyone know that Kerry has been having visions?"

"The killer watched us at the crime scene," Adrian said. "Or at least that's what Kerry felt."

Nate and Gage zeroed in on her. "You felt him there?" Gage asked. "When?"

"After everyone moved on to look for the woman. I just felt it for a moment. It didn't last long."

"Why didn't you say anything?" Gage asked.

Adrian stepped in. "She told me. But what were we gonna do? Call off the search for the wounded woman so we could hunt in the dark for a killer who didn't want to be found? I made a quick sweep of the area where she thought he might have been, but I didn't find anything. What was left to do, except search more closely at daylight, which you all did."

Nate seemed to agree with this, but he kept silent, deferring to Gage's official authority.

"Yeah," Gage said finally. "Yeah. You're right."

Adrian shook his head. "No, I was wrong. It was your decision to make, not mine. I'm a nobody in this. No authority."

Nate's attention shifted to Gage.

"This isn't about authority," Gage said flatly. "I invited you in on this, and as far as I'm concerned you have as much authority as anyone, just like Nate here. I agree we wouldn't have changed the search, so your decision was right. What wasn't right was that I never heard about it."

"It was just a feeling," Kerry said, feeling a need to defend Adrian, which surprised her. He seemed perfectly capable of defending himself. "And it only lasted a second or so. I wasn't even really sure of it."

"We've been running a lot on your feelings," he reminded her, "and they've turned out to be unbelievably accurate. So just don't keep them to yourself, okay?"

She nodded. "I hope to God I don't have another one."

Gage gave her a half smile. "I would have agreed with you until Adrian called. I was hoping this would be it, and we could settle down to finding our killer. Apparently there's going to be no time to settle down. Not with you in the crosshairs."

"How did she get in the crosshairs?" Nate asked.

"Because she was out at the scene," Gage began, then he paused. "I see what you mean."

"So do I," Adrian said.

Kerry spoke, tightening her hold on the afghan around her shoulders. "Will someone please enlighten *me*?"

Adrian spoke. "There'd be no reason to single you out unless someone fingered you as an informant."

Gage continued. "Exactly. Which means these guys are local, they're afraid someone else knows what they're up to."

"Unless," Nate observed, "someone has already put it out that you're psychic."

"But nobody except us knows that," Gage said. "I think we've been *very* careful with that."

"Except for one thing," Kerry said. "I stood at the scene and pointed out the direction the victim had fled. It was a fresh crime scene. We found no blood trail. No time for the killers to have talked to anyone. So how else could I know where she went, if not for my visions?"

"It's possible, I suppose," Gage agreed reluctantly. "But it's a big leap. It's not like we've ever relied on a psychic before."

"I'm not a psychic."

"At the moment," Adrian argued, "you seem to have been."

"Well, I hope that's the end of it." But did she really? After that call, shouldn't she be hoping she'd sense it if the killers came close to her? Dread, that damned presence, was beginning to sit on her shoulder again. Her heart sped up, uncomfortably so.

"We need to discuss the phone call," Gage said. "Did anything about it catch your attention? Accent? Voice? Background noise?"

Kerry shook her head. "Not really. The voice sounded fake. Like he was trying not to sound like himself. And he only said two words, so it wasn't like I had a lot of time." But the memory of those words sent a chill racing down her spine.

"It could also mean almost anything," Nate remarked. "They'd have to be fools to go after her now. She's been threatened and you're going to put a watch on her, right?"

"It's already been ordered," Gage said. "And Adrian's going to be with her every minute."

"Well, as a rule I've found criminals to be more stupid than they are smart. But this call was really stupid if he meant it. Anybody with two brain cells to rub together would know Kerry's going to have heavy protection after that."

"You'd think," Adrian agreed.

"So maybe," Gage suggested, "he just wants to scare her away from passing any more information." He looked at Adrian. "We'll have the autopsy and CSU prelims by noon tomorrow. Let me know whether you want to come by the office to see them, or have them brought over here. As for tracing the calls, the phone company doesn't keep records of local calls. All they can do is add a tap to your line to keep the numbers of future callers."

Nate and Gage departed a short time later. They didn't have a lot of facts about the case to discuss yet, and no one really felt like indulging in polite chitchat.

That left Kerry and Adrian sitting almost like mannequins in the living room, silent and unmoving.

"You must need some sleep," Kerry remarked when the silence grew too oppressive.

"I've been catnapping all day. I'm fine." He smiled but the expression didn't reach his eyes. "Don't answer your phone again," he suggested. "Let me get it for you."

"No!" The word burst out of her. She didn't even know where it came from, but it was as if a huge bubble of anger and resentment had been lying below the surface and suddenly found a way out.

"No," she repeated, throwing off the afghan and pacing the rug in her socks. "This is insane. I didn't ask for these visions or dreams or whatever they are. They just happened. But in two days, they've taken over my life. I can't go to school, I can't go out, I've got a live-in bodyguard and now I can't answer my phone? I don't think so!"

"Kerry..."

"Did I do anything wrong? Not that I can remember. I didn't commit a crime. In fact, I may have helped save a woman's life."

"There's no doubt about that," he said quietly.

"So why should I have to be locked up in my own house, cut off from even answering my own telephone?" She faced him, spreading her arms. "If you want to tap my telephone, fine. But I'm going to answer it when it rings, damn it. It's still my house and my phone!"

He was nodding. He didn't even smile, which might have led her to believe she was being ridiculous. In fact, he looked as if he understood completely.

Which rather took the wind out of her sails. You can't fight when no one fights back.

She continued pacing, circling the room, working off a burst of unpleasant energy. Cripes, she couldn't even go jogging now.

"How long is this going to last?" she asked the air. She didn't get an answer, nor did she expect one. There *was* no answer. As long as it takes, that was the answer.

Finally running down, she returned to the couch, tucking her legs beneath her and folding her arms across her breasts.

Adrian finally spoke. "It stinks," he agreed.

"Yeah, it does. But I'm acting like an idiot."

"No, you're not."

She glared at him. "Yes. I am. Things happen to people all the time, things they don't want. Like I have more to complain about than the woman in the hospital who was shot? Not likely."

"Feelings don't always give way to logic." He reached out and clasped her fisted hand. His hand was big and warm, even a bit callused, and she enjoyed its comforting touch. After a moment she opened her hand and turned it so that their fingers could clasp. He squeezed back.

"My girlfriends were supposed to come over for dinner tomorrow," she said presently. "I guess I'll have to call it off."

"Why?"

"Because I haven't done the shopping yet. Looks like I can't do it now. Besides, I'm not sure I'd want them to come over here. I'd feel like I might be drawing that madman's attention to them."

She could feel him hesitate. Big, strong and warm beside her on the couch, his grasp on her hand protective, he was still the kind of man who would actually think about how to enable some silly girls' get-together dinner. All the more impressive when he could just agree with her and tell her it was impossible.

Instead he said, "Let me think about. Maybe I can figure out how to make it happen."

She shook her head. "Thanks, Adrian, but I think it would be wiser to cancel it. Maybe we can do it next week."

"It's only temporary," he agreed.

She didn't think either of them believed it at that moment, though. They knew so little and the threat was so big. Who the hell would run around killing people for a *game*? She couldn't begin to imagine the mind-set, yet everything she had sensed so far had given her that impression of these men.

Needing something more stable than the strange

world she'd been inhabiting since yesterday morning, she turned a little and looked at Adrian.

He was already looking at her. She couldn't read his face. It seemed to be carved in stone, as if he were tightly holding something in check. But as their gazes met and held, something changed. The air seemed to lighten and sparkle.

Then, without a word, a question or a warning, he bent his head and kissed her.

Firm lips against soft lips. Just a gentle kiss, nothing more. Not even a hint of passion. Just...something kinder and even warmer.

When he slowly pulled back, his eyes were still fixed on her. The air seemed charged with expectation.

As Kerry continued to stare into his eyes, she felt little sparkles of excitement skipping around her nerve endings as if they wanted to wake her from the nightmare of the last two days. The sensation was delightful, more than she could ever have imagined from a mere touching of lips, but it was also powerful enough to focus every cell in her brain right here, right now, aware only of herself and Adrian a few inches away.

Her world, which had tipped too far into oppressive darkness, seemed to spring back a little, reminding her again that life was good.

She smiled and leaned back on the couch, choosing to rest her head on his shoulder. That didn't seem too forward after the kiss. A kiss that neither of them appeared to want to discuss. The touch had said everything for now.

"You asked about my accident yesterday," she said. "I didn't really answer."

"Well, you did. As much as anyone would want to tell a stranger, I suppose."

"After what you've seen in the last day or so, I don't feel like we're strangers anymore. You've had a clear look inside my warped psyche."

He stirred. "Who said it was warped?"

"Well, most people don't have visions like that."

"How would we know? Most people could have them and never tell anyone because they're afraid of being laughed at."

"I never thought of that possibility."

"Sometimes," he said, "you just know things. I know I do. Me, I call it hunches. Psychologists would say it's a combination of experience and fresh input, causing snap judgments that I don't have to think through. But sometimes it's a bit odder than that. I think it must be for everyone. But it's so easy to call it coincidence."

Kerry nodded, her cheek rubbing against his shoulder. "Yeah. That's what I always called it before. Mainly because it was nothing as big as this. Usually it was little stuff."

"Exactly. So who's to say this isn't just a normal thing blown larger than life?"

"You're so reassuring."

At that he gave a deep rumble of laughter. "Yeah, sure."

She smiled again, even though he couldn't see it, and tried to focus on the past, if for no other reason than to escape today for a little while.

"So what happened?" he prodded.

"Well, it was the end of winter break. A bunch of us had left our families a couple of days after Christmas to go skiing, and from there we were heading back to college. It was on the way back to school that it happened."

She closed her eyes, this part of it etched so vividly on her memory. "The roads weren't bad. The sun was out, it hadn't snowed in a couple of days. But we were busy chatting and laughing, and I guess my friend wasn't paying as close attention as she should have, because the snowmelt was running across the pavement, keeping large patches of it wet. Safe enough until she rounded a tight curve into the shadow of a mountain where the sun hadn't hit the road that morning. She should've seen it, would've seen it if the rest of us hadn't been carrying on like fools."

"That happens."

"So we hit that shaded spot and it hadn't thawed yet. Black ice covered the whole section of road, they told me later. All I remember is that suddenly we had no traction and were sliding across the road. We hit the guard rail and flipped and...I don't remember a thing after that. Apparently the car tumbled down a cliff about two hundred feet. Anyway, an EMT was behind us and saw it all happen. Unfortunately my girlfriends didn't make it. Both of them died at the scene."

"I take it you weren't much better?"

"Apparently not. I had a lot of injuries. Broken bones, cracked skull, a couple of fractured vertebrae. That's why they tell me I died twice before I reached the emergency room."

"Why did they tell you that?"

She moved her head, although not even she was sure if she meant it in denial or something else. "My parents told me. They'd been scared to death and it all just came bubbling out. But I already knew anyway."

"You *knew?*"

She sighed. "I knew. You see—" she gave a little laugh "—this is the point where a lot of people start to back away. Except for the ones who already believe and want to make me into something exceptional. I think the only evenhanded person I talked to about it was the hospital psychologist. She told me the experience was a common one, and until she had it herself, she wasn't going to judge it. She just said to take it for what it was, and if it changed me into a better person, as such experiences often did, then she certainly wasn't going to tell me I imagined it."

"Sounds like a smart lady."

"Very. She helped me through a lot, I can tell you. Right when I needed validation most, she was there."

She felt rather than saw his nod. "Anyway," she continued, "while I was supposedly dead, I was awake. That was the strangest part of it. My body was dead and I was outside it, watching. Detached. I even had the thought that that must be how a butterfly felt about its chrysalis."

"That's really something."

"Yeah. Anyway, I heard them say my heart had stopped, I watched them defib me, try to get me breathing, all of it. I knew it was me they were working on,

and I didn't especially care. Because there was something else. Something more important."

"And that was?"

"This feeling," she said. "This incredible feeling I
can't even begin to describe. Love, so much love. I felt
as if I were floating in a sea of it. And when I turned
away from my body, I saw this brilliant light. A light so
pure and crystalline I could almost touch it. And then I
was moving toward it faster and faster, and I saw people,
mostly silhouettes, but I knew them all. I even saw my
two friends who were in the car when we crashed. That's
when I knew they hadn't survived. I knew it, and I raced
toward them, wanting to hug them.

"But then I stopped. I couldn't fly forward anymore.
And Ginny, the girl who'd been driving, said, 'Kerry, it's
not time for you yet. You have to go back.'"

"I'm getting chills here," he said quietly.

"I do, too, at this part. I said I didn't want to go back.
But she said I had to, that I wasn't finished. But she
wouldn't tell me what I still had to do. The next thing I
knew, I was waking up in the emergency room, hurting
like hell, hearing people barking orders to one another.
Then, for an instant when I opened my eyes, it was as
if they all grew still. As if they didn't believe what they
were seeing. Next thing I remember, my gurney was
being rushed down a hallway. I guess that's when I went
to surgery."

"That is some story," he said quietly.

"Yeah." She sighed, closing her eyes again, reaching
back to the aftermath. "I felt so guilty that I was still

alive when my friends had died, but at the same time I felt so envious because I knew where they'd gone. It took me a while to work through all that."

"I would think so. Losing friends causes a lot of conflicting feelings."

"Exactly. In the end I was just glad I hadn't been driving. I think if I had been I never would have been able to handle it. But while I was feeling so guilty for surviving, the feeling of the light stayed with me. At first I was resentful that I'd been told to come back. Then I realized Ginny was right. For some reason I needed to stay here. And instead of being resentful, I started to carry a piece of that light inside me. A memory maybe, but a kind of guidepost, too."

"How do you mean?"

She tilted her head up and looked at him. "You can never forget being touched by that kind of love. And when you have been, you know what you need to give back to the world. There's no question after that."

His face had settled into a deeply thoughtful expression, as if he was internalizing what she had told him. She liked the way he responded, seriously, neither dismissing her nor lauding her. It was, after all, just an experience. It certainly didn't give her an edge, and it certainly didn't make her crazy. If anything, it had ratcheted up her conscience in unexpected ways.

Then of course, she had lost her fear of death, which made her a pretty odd bird in most circles. That didn't mean she would recklessly risk herself, but she honestly didn't spend a lot of time trying to avoid the inevitable.

She wasn't afraid, for example, to eat a strip of bacon or an egg when she felt like it, any more than she felt virtuous for eating a salad for dinner. Preoccupation with those things, so much a popular concern, seemed like a waste of time. Everything in moderation was her rule, and then forget about it.

The feeling extended throughout her life, focusing her attention on those matters she believed to be far more important, like the development of her students.

As she had once joked to a friend, God had thrown her back in the pond. Apparently she wasn't ready yet.

"You know," she said a couple of minutes later, "it's weird."

"What is?"

"These feelings I have that I have something I need to do before I die."

"I think a lot of people feel that way."

"Really?"

"Really. The need for purpose is a common human trait."

"Maybe so. But it takes on a little more meaning after you've been tossed back."

At that he chuckled. "I guess it would."

She gave a little laugh, too. "I don't mean to sound self-important. Because I really believe *everyone* has a purpose."

"I wasn't taking it that way."

"Good. But maybe what I'm trying to say is that I'm a little more fatalistic? Like, when my number is up it's up?"

"I can understand why you would feel that way."

"Yeah, I guess a lot of people do from what the psychologist said. But at the same time, it makes me more grateful. I'm not saying I'm perfect by any means. I still take things for granted. But it has certainly refocused me."

He touched her chin with his forefinger, gently lifting her face until they could look at each other. "You don't need to explain. I've got a pretty good idea what you're talking about. Part of the reason I retired was that I couldn't spend another day dealing with the underside. I needed to get into the fresh air and sunshine and remember that the world is a good place. Getting wounded was a good excuse."

"How badly were you hurt?"

"I've recovered." He withdrew his finger from her chin, making it clear he wasn't prepared to venture into that territory.

"You stay here for a few minutes," he said, rising. "And don't answer the phone."

"Where are you going?"

"I'm going to walk around outside and make sure everything's in place. Then I can doze off in a chair for a little while."

The door had shut, she realized. Whatever chasm they'd been crossing, the drawbridge had just closed with a loud bang.

Chapter 6

"That was a stupid move," the younger man said, his voice rising nearly an octave. His eyes had a wild look.

"Shut up and listen!"

"But that phone call warned them. They'll have cops all over her now."

"That was the point."

The younger man's jaw dropped. "You're crazy."

"I've been right so far, haven't I?"

The younger one nodded reluctantly. A kind of misery had framed his face, but there was something else there, too. Something excited.

"Listen," the older man said. "Hunting is great when the animal doesn't know you're there. But it's a helluva lot better when the quarry is on guard. Ready for you.

Ready to run. It's a bigger challenge and it makes it so much sweeter. Trust me, I know."

The younger man hesitated. His friend had been right about everything so far. And he had to admit he liked the power he'd felt when that woman's head had exploded. His only disappointment had been that it was too dark to chase the other one successfully.

"Okay," he said finally. "Okay. But you better have an idea how to do this."

"I have lots of ideas. One thing I know for sure is we can't go after anyone else until we get her out of the way. Not if what your friend told you is right."

"I'm not sure he knows what he's talking about. It sounds so crazy. Besides, even he thought it was a pile of crap."

"Except that she was there. You saw her. And they listened to her."

The young guy shrugged. "Yeah, I guess."

"So she's next. And we'll do it together."

At that the younger one seemed to brighten. It didn't sound so impossible now.

In the morning after breakfast, Kerry called her friends to postpone the weekly dinner. All of them were understanding but Joyce and Marybeth wanted to come over anyway.

"Please don't," Kerry begged. "I don't want you to get into the middle of this."

"In the middle of what, for heaven's sake?" Joyce

said. She was always the most assertive of the group, ever since they'd met in kindergarten.

"I can't tell you," Kerry said firmly. "I can't. All I know is that you'll be in danger."

Joyce fell silent for several long seconds. Finally, "Kerry, are you in trouble?"

"Not in any way you can help. Honestly. The sheriff is taking care of everything. I just don't want you all involved in any way."

"That's not how our gang works, Kerry."

"It has to this time. It *has* to. If you come over here, things might get worse."

That was the argument that silenced Joyce at last. "All right. But when this is all over I expect every single detail."

"I promise."

When she replaced the receiver in the cradle once again, she turned to find Adrian standing in the doorway, arms folded as he leaned against the frame. "You have some very loyal friends."

"I'm very lucky. We've been friends since we were little kids."

He arched a brow. "Always?"

Kerry had to smile. "Oh, there were times we went our separate ways. Plenty of them. College was the longest. But we always get back together again. It's like gravity. You're eventually going to come back to earth."

"That's pretty special."

"Yes, it is."

"How are you doing?"

Her smile faded about two degrees. "Well, there are lots of ways I could answer. I'm well. I hate being locked up like this. I'm worried that I may not be able to get back to work on Monday. I'm disappointed I can't have my friends over, and I think I already have a touch of cabin fever."

"That's pretty encompassing." He smiled broadly.

"So which 'doing' did you want to know about?"

At that he laughed. "Okay. I got my answer."

She joined his laughter. "Sorry, I was being a pain. I'm always telling my students to be as specific as possible in their writing. Not to leave room for doubts or confusion. And since I spend all my professional time hammering that, I'm probably too sensitive to ordinary courtesy questions."

"I wasn't just being courteous. I really wanted to know. On the other hand, I wasn't expecting a verbal joust."

She laughed again. "Good luck. You can take the teacher out of the school but you can't take the school out of the teacher."

His shoulders shook with amusement. "I imagine you can't stand the question 'How are you?'"

"Now there's an open-ended one. Do you take it as a question about the general state of your life or only your existence at that particular moment? Either way, nobody wants a real answer."

"Yeah, just the 'I'm fine, and you?'"

"Exactly. So when some of my students argue those things against me when I demand specificity, I tell them there's a whole lot of difference between a courtesy that helps grease the cogs of society, and writing a paper or trying to make a point."

"Good point, teacher."

She gave a mock bow. "Thank you."

The wind chose that moment to gust against the side of the house. Old wood creaked an aged protest, and in places the curtains stirred as air snaked through hidden cracks. Just as the house stopped creaking, the sunny day darkened. A cloud had moved overhead.

"This is one of the things I love most about autumn," Kerry confided. "The way the weather can be so changeable. One minute bright sun, the next a cloud darkens things."

"Does that fireplace in the living room work?"

"Actually, yes. I had the chimney cleaned a couple of months ago, too."

"Wood?"

"There's a stack by the back door."

"Then what do you say we light a fire? The weather forecast is for cold and rain."

"That does sound cozy. Should I make hot chocolate or soup?"

"Maybe later. Let me get the fire going first. Then we can watch a movie or play cards."

He was trying to entertain her, she thought. Then she realized she wasn't the only one trapped in this house for the duration. They both needed a break.

Deciding it might be time for some B movie with lots of monsters and plenty of unintended laughs, she went to search her DVD collection. There could, she reasoned, be some good points to being locked up in her house with an attractive man.

It was certainly something she hadn't tried in a long time.

Rain fell steadily, heavily. Thunder rumbled in the distance but never seemed to draw closer. Inside, with a nice fire and *Tremors* on the TV screen, life seemed pretty good.

It seemed even better to be holding hands, and Kerry wished she had the nerve to press the issue further, like turning into him and kissing him. Instead she kept her gaze trained on the screen and tried not to notice how good he smelled, and how beckoning his body heat seemed.

She could, she thought, develop a real crush on this man. Unfortunately, that would be unwise until she found out what was behind that door he had slammed shut.

Not that her hormones cared. Heck no. They'd have been happy with a rough and ready tumble in the hay. Right now, they kept her in a state just below true arousal, somewhere around a tentative range that would take only one spark to set off the blaze. Every now and then she had to recross her legs to try to minimize the subtle ache at her center.

He was so attractive, she thought dreamily, forgetting everything else for now. So attractive. The aromas of man and soap combined into a heady mixture, and the feeling of calm strength he exuded called to her.

Only when you've been on your own for a long time, she realized, could you truly appreciate what it felt like to not be alone. Or could you truly realize how nice it could be to let someone else take charge for a bit.

She didn't feel weak or anything. But she liked being able to let go of the burdens for a bit. Liked forgetting every damn thing, knowing the man beside her was there to protect her from disaster. A brief break on the road of her life, to be sure, but one she welcomed.

It was, she thought with an inner laugh, almost like abandoning adulthood for a while.

But no, that definitely wasn't her, and besides, what she was feeling right now classified as adult. Definitely adult. R-rated. Potentially X-rated.

She stole a glance at him from the corner of her eye. He certainly seemed to be involved in the movie. That was fine, but at the moment she wished she'd picked something else. Something a little more suggestive. Something that fit her tingling nerve endings better.

A gust of wind rattled the windows again, another rumble of thunder in the distance. If there was any lightning, it failed to penetrate the heavy curtains.

"I love this movie," Adrian remarked with a laugh as it neared its climax. "I never get tired of it."

And something rattled at the windows.

At once Adrian stood up, movie forgotten. "Stay right here," he said. "I'm going to check things out."

She realized he was hyper-alert, more than she would have expected, actually. Yes, she'd had a threatening phone call, but Gage had put deputies on watch, and surely Adrian or she would hear if anyone tried to get inside.

So why was he so edgy?

Something rattled against the front window again, and she thought it sounded like sleet. She wanted to look but restrained herself. And at that instant she realized this situation would become intolerable before long. Not able to look out her window to check the weather? Not able to pop out to the store when she felt like it? Watched every minute?

But she'd already had her little temper tantrum. Having another would be beyond childish. Besides, all she had to do was remember what she had seen in her visions and in the woods to know there was no room right now for irresponsibility or childishness.

But that didn't mean she had to like it.

The petulant thought leavened her mood a bit, and while the rattling against her window intensified, and the wind decided to imitate a banshee, she listened to Adrian's footsteps as he moved through her house.

When he returned she raised a brow. "So, did anything unlock itself?"

For an instant he appeared taken aback, then he gave a laugh. "No, of course not. I was just being extra cautious. It's sleeting. Maybe we should check the weather."

She flipped to the weather station with its familiar faces and they waited for the local forecast. Winter was moving in almost before autumn had begun. Snow was on tap for the night.

She looked at Adrian. "That's good, isn't it?"

"I think so. We've already warned people to stay out of the woods, but the snow should deter even the diehards."

Kerry nodded agreement. "I think we can take a

breath and relax." Rising, she announced she was hungry. "I'm going to go make us something. Any preferences?"

"Whatever you feel like."

In the kitchen, by herself at least for a minute or two, she opened the refrigerator door and tried to decide what she could make easily and quickly that wasn't a frozen dinner. At the moment, she was low on supplies, as it was just about time for her to do her weekly shopping.

Finally she settled for heating a couple of cans of chili—always good on a cold night—and dressing it up with some cheese and tortilla chips. Sleet battered the windows periodically, sounding like the rattle of claws.

All of a sudden she felt uncomfortable. It was as if something dark had moved into her kitchen, something just beyond the reach of her five senses. Ordinarily this was about the coziest room in the house, but right now it didn't feel cozy at all.

She grabbed a tray and carried the supper out to the living room where she set up wooden TV tables for each of them. With the fire burning cheerfully, the uneasiness that had found her in the kitchen drew away. The chili was warm and satisfying in a way only a few things could be on a cold stormy night. Like a warm blanket, but on the inside.

The weather still filled the TV screen, but the muted audio got lost in the sounds of the crackling fire and the wind outside.

Kerry spoke. "It must have been something, working for the department."

"Why do you say that?"

"Well, it's sort of like the state FBI, right?"

"In some ways. But this is Wyoming, remember?"

At that she laughed. "But we have our own share of crime. Admit it."

"That's true. Just on a smaller scale usually."

"Well, we wouldn't need them if local police could handle everything."

He looked amused. "What do you want to know?"

"Oh, I don't know. What the work was generally like."

"We helped local law enforcement a lot in counties where they couldn't afford all the bells and whistles. We joined investigations that crossed county lines. And occasionally we had some really big stuff, like rustling."

She nodded. "I think you're minimizing your role."

"I think I'm not blowing it out of proportion."

She laughed. "Okay, okay."

"A lot of it was pretty humdrum, Kerry. Most investigations are. If you followed the average investigator for a month, you wouldn't get half the excitement you can get on a TV show. In fact, you might mistake us for clerks."

"Oh, come on..."

"I kid you not. You talk to a lot of people, you take a lot of notes, you spend hours on the phone and you try to put puzzle pieces together. That's most of it. Once in a great while you get something much bigger. Like the time a few years back when we learned that cocaine was being shipped in cattle trucks, buried under the manure."

"Oh! I think I remember that!"

"It was interesting enough to make the news," he agreed. "You know how bad a cattle truck smells."

"Oh, yeah. I was picnicking at a rest stop one afternoon on my way to Helena to visit a friend. Just as I started eating my sandwich, a cattle truck pulled in."

He laughed. "I feel oodles of sympathy."

"You should. My God, the stench. The place was basically just a roadside turnout with a couple of tables. I still don't know why that trucker had to stop *there*. But he did and I couldn't even swallow. So I left and waited until I got to Helena to eat."

"It's certainly a rich aroma. But that was basically the idea. Haul the cows and the coke across the Canadian border, and cover any possible scent the K-9's might detect with that wonderful, unforgettable...aroma."

"Did it work?"

"Nobody even thought of it until we got a tip. That's when the fun began. We had to find a cattle truck that was actually transporting the stuff."

"Oh, Lord."

"Exactly. It was definitely a...crappy job."

She laughed. "So how'd you solve it?"

He gave a quiet chuckle. "Out tipster got us information on a specific shipment. Thank God. I thought I was never going to get the smell of those trucks out of my nose."

She joined his laughter. "But what a clever idea!"

"It was. It most definitely was. But after we stopped that one truck we found out something fascinating."

"Which was?"

"The dogs could still smell the cocaine. Despite all that overriding odor. Most amazing thing I ever saw."

"Dogs are incredible."

"I couldn't agree more. I got to thinking it was like a partnership. The dogs made up for our lacks. We see better, but they smell so much better."

"Sometimes, too, I think we get misled by our eyes."

"Yeah, we do. But it's not easy to mislead a dog with odors."

The wind whistled with renewed strength and they paused, listening.

"I'm glad I don't have to go out tonight," Kerry said. "It sounds unfriendly out there."

"Decidedly so."

That's when she realized that dark feeling was coming back, the one she'd had in the kitchen. What was going on? She'd always been perfectly comfortable in this house. Even all alone, everything seemed welcoming.

But tonight... Tentatively she looked at Adrian. "I'm feeling something," she told him hesitantly.

He cocked a brow. "Feeling something?"

"Something...dark. It's making me uneasy, silly as it sounds."

"After the last two days, nothing you feel sounds silly to me. Can you figure out what it is?"

"No. I don't like it. I felt it in the kitchen while I was heating the chili, but when I came in here it was gone. Now it's coming back."

He moved his table to one side, meal half eaten. "I'm

going to check outside. Lock the door after me, and resist any urge to look out, okay?"

"Adrian..."

"It'll be okay. Trust me. Just do what I said."

Chapter 7

Not that he trusted himself all that much, he thought as he pulled on his jacket and shoved his feet into his boots. But he also couldn't trust anyone else. He'd learned that lesson the hard way. When you couldn't even trust your own partner, who could you trust?

He stepped out the front door into the early autumn night and the gale, waiting until he heard the lock turn behind him. Sleet stung his cheeks, and an unusual icy rime was beginning to build on tree branches. Not normal weather at all for this part of the world. Usually it was too dry here for this, and dryer than ever when it grew cold.

Street lights danced off the building ice, giving the world a glittery look. The wind had ripped most of the leaves off the deciduous trees in just the last couple of hours, leaving bony, icy fingers behind, and only a few hangers-on.

The deputy's car was still parked two houses down, in a puddle of darkness between two street lights. He doubted the guy was even getting out of his car to walk around now. This was a night for all living things to find shelter. Still, he'd have to say something.

He stepped off the porch and began to walk around the outside of the house. It was darker, of course, once he left the front, but he was glad to see that little light emerged from the house in cracks around the heavy curtains. It wouldn't be easy to guess where Kerry was by the lights. And it would be impossible to look in.

The browning grass, icy now, crunched beneath his boots. Silent approach had become impossible. He paused frequently to listen, but little could be heard over the wind. Another spray of sleet stung his cheek and caused him to close one eye.

It only took him ten minutes to walk around the house slowly, checking every shadowed spot. Nobody had been out here since the sleet had started though. His own footprints were as clear as neon signs right now.

No one was out here. No one. He headed down the street to the patrol car, bent on asking the deputy why he hadn't taken a walk around like he was supposed to. He could understand not wanting to get out of a warm car in this weather, but the man still had an assignment to perform.

His long strides carried him past the front porch of

Kerry's house just as she flung it open and called his name. He whirled at once.

"I thought I told you to stay inside."

"Something's wrong, Adrian. Terribly wrong. I can feel it growing."

Words seemed to fail her at that point. He looked at her figure, silhouetted against the bright doorway, the sleet catching fire as the light struck it.

"Get inside and close the door," he ordered her. "No arguments. I'm on it."

To his vast relief, she obeyed him, closing the door with a thud. He thought he heard the snick of the lock.

No one appeared to be out in this miserable weather. From end to end, the street seemed empty except for parked cars. Even the shadows had lost some of their depth and darkness as the sleet splintered and spread the light around.

Shouldn't the deputy have at least gotten out of his vehicle to see what Adrian was doing prowling in the yard?

Dread, no stranger to a cop, returned to its familiar perch at the edges of his mind. When he reached the driver's side of the car, he couldn't see anything inside. The windows were steaming up, including the windshield. What the hell? Why didn't the guy have the defroster on?

He pounded on the window, feeling the stirrings of an anger he hadn't felt for a couple of years now. Not since that night in Gillette... He brushed the thought away and pounded on the window again.

"Deputy!"

Finally the window started to roll down and he found himself looking into a young, drowsy face.

"Have you been sleeping?"

A shame-faced look answered him. "I didn't mean to. The last thing I knew I was awake...."

Adrian stifled a frustrated sound and bent down to look straight in at the guy. "If you can't stay awake, call for a replacement. If somebody goes for the teacher tonight and you're asleep, they might take you out, too."

At that the young man completely woke up. His eyes were suddenly wide and clear.

"Now get out of the car, lock it and come for a walk around with me. It'll get your blood stirring. Then call for relief and stay awake until it gets here. Got me?"

The man nodded. He rolled up the window, then climbed out of the car and locked it.

"Let's go," Adrian said. "Something's wrong, and I'm not sure it was just you sleeping."

"I'm sorry," the younger man said. "I can't believe I did that."

"It's easy with the car heater on," Adrian said a bit more amiably. "Stakeouts are hard at the best of times." He looked at the deputy as they walked toward the yard. "Cal, isn't it?"

"Yes, sir."

"We'll pretend this didn't happen."

"Thanks. I appreciate it."

"Okay," Adrian said, stopping them at the driveway.

"The only footprints in the yard around the house should be mine. I followed a pretty straight path, so they won't be scattered around. If you notice anything else, sound out."

"I will."

At that moment, a dog down the street started barking, penetrating the otherwise quiet night.

Adrian stiffened, and felt Cal do the same.

"Cat?" asked Cal.

"I don't know. Let's keep together and make a quick tour around." He was rewriting the plan in his mind quickly. "Then we're going to go inside together. You can call for backup from there."

Cal paused midstride and looked at him. "You think something's wrong."

"Didn't I say so? Call it a hunch. Something's not right."

Another dog took up the frenzied barking of the first, this one closer. That did it. Adrian decided to skip circling the house again. Instead he motioned Cal to the porch and knocked. "Kerry? It's me."

An instant later the door opened and she peered out. "What's going on?" she asked as she saw Cal.

"I don't know." He looked at the deputy. "Get inside. Kerry, put on that vest. Cal, show her how. I'm going to look around some more."

"But..." Kerry didn't look as if she liked this.

Adrian shook his head. "You said something was wrong. I feel it, too. Now just do what I asked, would you?"

As soon as she nodded, he closed the door on both of them. "Lock it," he said. He heard the bolt snap into place.

Then, reaching under his jacket, he felt for the snub-nosed .38 he carried everywhere, because once you'd been a lawman, there was always someone who wanted to get you. It was usually invisible under jackets and sweatshirts, except at the height of a summer day. Most people probably never even guessed he went every-where armed.

Revolver in hand, he started once again to circle the house, listening to the dogs, trying to discern their message. When another one started barking, he froze in his steps, sleet stinging his face, listening intently. On a night like this, dogs should be inside. Some people had apparently forgotten that.

But were they just stirring each other up? Or were they reporting a prowler? More than once in his life he had wished dogs could talk. They perceived a different world, and much more acutely than any human could.

By the time he had circled the house again, the barking had begun to abate. Either owners were rescuing their animals from the cold, or the disturbance had passed.

He still didn't like it.

Returning to the front of the house, he climbed onto the porch and stood scanning the neighborhood. Sleet sparkled in the air like falling diamonds, but nothing in the shadows moved. Finally he turned and knocked. Cal let him in.

Kerry sat on the sofa, wearing the vest, looking half disgruntled and half frightened.

"Nothing out there that I could see," he said.

"Can I take this thing off now?"

He cocked his head to one side, rising on his toes to try to restore circulation to them, and half smiling at her. "You said something was wrong. Do you still feel that way?"

She hesitated, then shook her head. "I don't feel anything anymore."

"Good. 'Cause I don't feel anything in my feet, either. It's cold out there."

That evoked a smile from her. He looked at Cal. "Did you call for relief?"

He nodded. "Should be here in fifteen minutes or so."

"Good. Go ahead and relax until he gets here."

"I can't figure why I dozed off like that," Cal said. "I'm usually a night owl. That's why I volunteer for night shifts all the time."

Kerry spoke kindly, even as she was trying to undo the Velcro tapes holding the vest in place. "We're all a little wired and tired after the last couple of days, Cal. Darn, this thing is heavy."

"But warm," Adrian observed.

She scowled at him, but then a little laugh emerged. "True. I'm certainly not cold."

He bent over and helped her yank the tapes. Armor was something you had to don and doff a couple of times before you got used to the method, even though it was basically simple. Then he helped lift it over her head and put it on the couch beside her.

"I can't imagine having to work in one of those!"

Both men answered at the same time. "You get used to it."

"I guess."

Adrian saw her try to smile, but the brief moments of humor had fled. He could certainly understand why. The lurking horror didn't leave room for much else.

A knock on the door summoned him, and he opened it to find Deputy Virgil Beauregard waiting. Beau, as he was called by friends, had been on the force long enough to considerably relieve Adrian's concerns.

"I'm here to take over," Beau said in his easy drawl. He looked past Adrian. "You go on home, Cal. The roads are getting really dangerous."

"Thanks, Beau," Cal said as he slipped past the two men. "It's an awful night."

"Worse than awful," Beau remarked. He pulled the fur collar of his heavy jacket up tighter around his neck. As soon as Cal got into his car, he returned his attention to Adrian.

"I don't know if that boy has what it takes. It's not that damn late."

"I know. But he's still young."

"Young enough to get his butt killed." Beau shook his head. "I walked around the house. Two sets of footprints. Yours?"

"Mine."

"Okay. I'll be in the car if you need me."

Kerry had come up beside Adrian. "Do you need any coffee or food?"

Beau smiled at that. "Ma'am, my wife sent me out with enough coffee and food to get me through a week." He touched the brim of his hat. "Have a good night." He turned to go back to his car.

Adrian waited until he saw the deputy get safely inside his vehicle, and only then closed and locked the door.

"I feel better about that," he remarked.

"He's a good deputy," Kerry agreed. "He's always been great about coming to the school and talking about law as a career field. The students really like him."

"I don't know him all that well, but from what I've seen he seems to be capable and levelheaded."

"I agree with that."

The conversation tapered off, though. There seemed to be little to say, possibly because there was little enough they could think about except the killings and the threat against her.

But it was all she could think about, her brain running like a hamster on a wheel.

She shook her head, clearly not really meaning anything by it, perhaps responding to the entire situation. "I don't get it."

"Get what?"

"Why this happened. Why *I* had those visions. What good did they really do?"

"How can you ask that? Without you, we'd never have found that woman in time. She would have died out there one way or another. We've already discussed this."

Her head jerked a little. "You're right. I'm being selfish."

"I can sure understand why. Nothing wrong with it. I get selfish, too."

She looked at him, one corner of her mouth lifted, though it was a poor attempt at a smile. He felt something in his chest tighten, and he wished he could wave his hand and erase her worry. "Nooo," she said sarcastically.

"Yesss," he repeated in the same tone, then shrugged. "I didn't want to be responsible for your safety."

She started to stiffen, and he was certain she would tell him to leave then, but he squeezed her hand. "Not because of *you*," he said quickly. "Because it scared me."

She turned a little to see him better, but left her hand in his as if she took comfort from it. "Really?"

"Really." He hesitated., wondering why he felt compelled to bring this up now. All he knew was that he needed for her to understand him better. At the moment, with the words hovering on his lips, he didn't want to think about what that might mean. It was enough that at some level he needed her to know. Needed to make a connection with her that he had long refused to make with anyone else. The words nearly erupted from that need.

He said, "I don't tell many people about what happened, but it wasn't just a wound that made me take early retirement."

"No?" Her expression grew intent, caring.

"No. There was something else." He shook his head. "Sorry, I still find it hard to talk about, although I'm not sure why. Basically what happened was that I had an informant. He called me in a panic, telling me they were after him, that I had to pull him in before they killed him.

So I headed over to his place, and had a flat tire on the way. I'll never forget how impatient I got. It wasn't like I was somewhere I could just call a cab. We were out in ranch country. Anyway, I changed the damn tire as fast as I could, cursing all the while, then floored the car to get to his house."

"You were too late." She squeezed his hand and held on tight.

"Worse than that. I was barely too late. And because of that I found out my partner was in league with the bad guys. He had just killed my informant when I walked in. After that...well, it's a blur, but my partner's dead and I was wounded pretty badly. I just managed to call for help."

She nodded slowly, holding his gaze. "So he betrayed you, and you failed your informant."

"Basically, yeah."

But the description, accurate as it was, failed to convey the emotional reality of it. "I was a mess for a while, and not just from the bullet. My *partner*, for the love of heaven. My partner. The informant trusted me, and all the while the guy I trusted with my life was a traitor. So my informant, hardly more than a kid really, maybe twenty-two, was dead because he trusted me."

"You can't blame yourself for that."

"Logically, no. Emotionally is a very different thing."

She nodded slowly and laid her other hand on his knee. "I can understand that."

"Can you?" A harsh, bitter laugh escaped him. "I'm not sure I do. Anyway, when Gage asked me to stay with you I couldn't quite...feel comfortable about it."

"You're afraid you'll fail me, too."

"Of course I am. And now we're looking at a situation where someone may have said something they shouldn't have, which put you at risk."

"The nightmare all over again."

His chest had squeezed tight, but he refused to give in to the welter of emotions that wanted to overcome him. Her voice and face conveyed such sympathy for him that he almost felt embarrassed.

"I don't want to be a baby about it," he said after a few beats.

"I don't think you're anywhere near being a baby about it. Once burned is twice shy, cliché or not. And you got a double burn. There'd be something wrong with you if you weren't uncomfortable having to protect me in this situation."

"Maybe so." He still felt as low as chicken droppings, though.

"No maybe about it. To this day I avoid driving on mountain roads in the winter. I'm so scared of black ice even thinking about it makes my heart race. We're getting to the time of year when I become a homebody. No, I'm not afraid of dying. But I *am* afraid of having another accident. Does that make sense?"

"It does to me." Without giving it a thought, he leaned back on the couch and slipped his arm around her. It felt good when she leaned into him and put her head on his shoulder. How long had it been since he had held a woman like this? A long time. Too long. Had he been avoiding women to punish himself?

The question caught him unawares, and for an instant he had that odd feeling of standing outside himself, seeing himself from a different point of view—a perspective so different that it approached a complete personality shift.

"Adrian?"

He looked at her.

"Are you okay?"

He realized that his momentary start must have conveyed itself to her. "Just reevaluating something about myself."

She nodded and snuggled her head against his shoulder, leaving him with his thoughts.

How many women in his life had been willing to do that? he wondered. Not many, if any. Just as men wanted a solution to every problem, women seemed to want an emotional therapy session that picked over every detail as if that would make it better.

Not this one. She seemed to understand that when he was ready he would speak...or not.

Oddly comforted by the simple offer of quiet companionship, he lowered his head to one side until it rested against her silky dark hair. She smelled so good. With that thought, he closed his eyes and gave himself up to the moment.

There were times, he thought, when it felt sufficient just to be alive.

Kerry would have thought it impossible, after sleeping so late, and with so much tension, to doze off. But somehow with Adrian's arm around her, she did just that.

Dreams came, pleasant ones and silly ones, fleeting and never to be remembered. But then something else started creeping in at the edges. Even in her sleep she tried to batter the darkness back.

But it would not go away, and as it grew denser and began to take over, she became restless.

Finally a voice plucked her out of the morass.

"Kerry." It was Adrian. "Kerry, wake up. You're having a bad dream."

Her eyes popped open, taking in the warmly lit living room, the fire in the fireplace, the familiar surroundings. Instead of comforting her, they disturbed her. As if they were a mirage behind which evil dwelled.

"God!" she said, shaking her head to free herself from the lingering tendrils of her nightmare. "Oh, God."

"What?"

"It's there again. I hate this."

"What?"

"The feeling in my dream. Something's going to happen. And I don't want to know about it!"

His other arm closed around her and held her tight. She burrowed into the comfort his warm strength offered, and tried not to let the darkness in.

Outside the storm howled. Sleet still rattled against the windows, portending an ice storm of record severity. No one, she thought, no one could get around in this. Not even the killers. For tonight everyone should be safe.

But it didn't feel that way to her.

Words escaped her before she even knew what they would be. "Is that woman we found under police protection in the hospital?"

"I don't know." Adrian grew tense against her. Then he dropped one arm from her and fished in his pocket, pulling out a cell phone.

The county had repeaters everywhere these days, but apparently the reception was poor tonight. Very poor. At last he gave up and used the land line.

"Gage?"

Kerry listened as she wrapped her arms around herself, as if her own embrace could block out the ugliness.

"Is that woman we found in the woods under protection? Kerry's worried about her."

Silence except for the rattling of ice.

"Okay, thanks."

He replaced the handset in the cradle and returned to her side. "He said he pulled the deputy who was watching her because there've been a pile of accidents on the state highway, and they asked the hospital staff to be alert to anyone approaching her room. But he's sending someone now."

She nodded, feeling like her neck had stiffened and the movement was too much to ask. She tried to tell herself that the stiffness came from the position she had slept in, but instead of lessening, it seemed to be growing.

"I want this to stop." It was unclear even to her whether she spoke to Adrian, or to the universe at large. "It *has* to stop."

"I agree. All of it. The murders, your visions... You can't keep up this way."

She looked at him then, a sinking feeling in the pit of her stomach. "But maybe I have to. Maybe that's what it's all about."

"What's all about?"

"My near-death experience. The strange premonitions I've had for so long. My quirks, as I called them. Maybe it all was to make this happen."

"But why?"

"That's asking too much," she sighed. "Do we really have to know the *why*? Sometimes I think *that* part is way beyond our comprehension."

"Well, it probably is."

She nodded, then leaned back against the cushion. "It's one of those things where we just have to trust."

Trust. That was a word that nearly made him shudder. Some betrayals were so huge that you couldn't trust ever again. Certainly not without a fight.

Being a cop required a certain natural level of suspicion, but he'd gone way past that since Barry's betrayal. Way past. He ought to be able to get over it. People got over things like that all the time. Divorced people, for example. Was his situation so much worse?

Somebody had died because of it.

Could that and that alone be enough? Or was he simply refusing to let go of the wound, instead choosing to hide behind a high emotional wall so that it could never happen again?

Probably the latter, he thought grimly. Nor was that necessarily foolish on his part.

Yet look at him now, thrust into a similar position with this woman, thanks to Gage, who knew exactly what he was asking of Adrian. Well-meaning friends and all that.

Hell.

But after finding Cal napping instead of keeping watch, he knew he couldn't walk away from this. He didn't trust anyone but himself. A sorry situation, one just confirmed by Cal's slip.

What an irony.

Needing to move, to expend some tension, he rose and went to peek out the front window, moving the curtain only marginally. The night outside had gone far past the glitter of falling diamonds. He could see now that ice rimed the bare tree branches in thick layers.

"This could be really bad," he remarked.

"What?"

"This storm. The ice is building on the branches of the trees. Most likely on power lines, too. We'd better gather up candles and figure out how to stay warm."

"I've got plenty of wood out back."

"Then I'll bring some in while you put together candles and flashlights. Then I think we need to make a bed for you right in front of the fire. On the couch."

"Maybe I should get out the air mattress."

He turned in time to see her rising from the couch, and again felt that odd squeezing in his chest as he noted her innate grace, noted once again how pretty she was. No matter how broken he might be, he was still a man, and the sight of her awakened his appetites.

Bad timing, he told himself. Bad, bad timing. "Yeah," he said. "That would be good."

Chapter 8

In the kitchen, Kerry hunted up every candle she had, and the two flashlights along with spare batteries. Power outages were usually a spring or summer thing around here, when severe thunderstorms and tornadoes blew through. The winters usually didn't get bad enough in terms of snow and ice to slow things down too much.

But that had been changing, she reminded herself. What had once been a fairly dry climate had grown increasingly wetter, and storms more severe. She understood you weren't supposed to generalize about the climate from short-term experience, but people who lived close to the earth and depended on the climate noted long-term changes more quickly than city dwellers.

Ranchers around here talked frequently about the changing climate, commenting on the increasing number of severe storms, on how it rained more often, how they'd been steadily adjusting their practices to the changes.

So now an ice storm unlike anything she'd seen in her entire thirty years in this county.

Maybe she'd assign a climate essay after all, asking students to write about their parents' and grandparents' perception of changes in the climate. That could be interesting for them and for her.

Adrian passed her several times with armloads of wood as she moved necessities to the living room. It would be cozy in there no matter what happened. A couple of oil lamps sat on her bedroom dresser, and she decided to bring them out, too. She seemed to remember having a bottle of lamp oil in the cabinet.

Every blanket she had, all the spare pillows... The living room soon looked more like a nest. Adrian inflated the air mattress with her blow-dryer, then together they made up beds. In the background, the TV still flickered, but with the sound off.

"Okay," she said when they were done. "All we need is popcorn."

"For what?"

"For the pajama party."

He chuckled. "I've never been to one."

"Now that's a pity! I'll have to introduce you."

He pretended to frown. He was kneeling on the floor beside the air mattress while she sat on the edge of the couch. "This isn't supposed to be fun," he said mock-sternly.

"Well, I don't see any point in being miserable on principle."

At that his frown quivered, trying to turn into a smile. "You're a hedonist."

"No such thing."

"You could fool me." He surprised her by holding out his hand. She didn't even hesitate, but took it. He squeezed, then astonished her by tugging her forward onto the air mattress. A second later he was lying beside her, propped on an elbow to look down at her.

"So," he said, his voice a trace husky, "tell me about this pajama-party thing. What did you girls do?"

"We giggled a lot." She felt as if she couldn't quite catch her breath, and the feeling grew stronger when he rested his hand on her midriff. The warm, light pressure felt *so* good.

"About what?"

"About everything." Closing her eyes, she cast her mind back in time. "About boys, about each other, about silly games we played. There wasn't much that didn't make us giggle. We'd get excited just being together."

"Sounds like I missed a great thing."

"Poor man." She opened her eyes and smiled at him. "It would have driven you crazy at that age. All those girls being silly over stupid things."

"Like guys weren't being silly over stupid things at the same age."

"Different things, though."

He shook his head, smiling. "Actually, it was probably about the same kind of stuff, except that we took ourselves oh-so seriously."

"I sort of remember that part."

"I certainly do."

His face seemed to have come closer, and Kerry held her breath, forgetting everything except a sudden, intense hope that he would kiss her. The power of the need swamped her, even as some corner of her heart wondered how she could feel something so innately fragile at a time like this...because all such things were fragile in the end. The powerful urge today could easily be gone tomorrow.

But she didn't care. As he lowered his head, she closed her eyes and waited for the touch of his lips, feeling as if every cell within her strained to reach him.

Then she felt the warm touch on her mouth, a gentle touch, asking, not demanding.

Almost without being aware of it, she raised her arms and placed her hands on his shoulders, opening herself completely to the moment. *Yesss!*

He took the invitation, his lips deepening the kiss, one arm slipping beneath her back to draw her closer.

That's what she wanted, she thought, to feel him all along the length of her body. To feel the warmth, the heat of desire, and through it the wonder of being alive. She needed that desperately right now. Needed *him* desperately right now.

The savagery of the need astonished her even as it swept her away. Elemental.

His tongue found hers in a dance of promise. It drove heat through her to her very center, until she felt herself throb inside in time to his thrusts. No one in her life had ever taken her so far so fast.

She felt him harden against her, a sensation that filled her with fierce pleasure. He felt it, too.

Then his hand slipped to her breast, a touch so light through the fabric that she shivered as much in anticipation as response. Ah, it was so good to be alive!

The crackle of the fire blended into the sounds of the ice storm without, creating a cocoon of sound around them, punctured only by sighs, and soon soft moans.

When her shirt started to ride up, and his hand moved with it, warm against the skin of her midriff, coming closer and closer to her breasts, she caught her breath, hoping against hope that he would not stop.

But he teased her for a little while, changing his kisses to gentle sips, like a bee tasting nectar, while his hand made slow circles on her skin. Then he dropped kisses across her cheek until he placed one on the tender spot behind her ear. At the same moment his warm breath puffed in her ear, and a shiver of delight shook her from head to foot.

A quiet, satisfied chuckle escaped him as he read her response as encouragement to continue.

Which it was. Her mind had gone hazy, able to think of only one thing... if that was even thinking. A groan rose deep from within her as she pulled him even closer, feeling that if she could fuse them into one it still wouldn't be enough.

A thrill ripped through her as her front-clasp bra gave way, allowing her to spill free. Then his hand found and cupped one breast. Warm. Hot. Hot as flame, shooting burning desire throughout her body.

When his thumb brushed her hardening nipple she arched against him and tightened her hold on his shoulders desperately.

Let it never end. Never.

His mouth replaced his thumb, sucking deeply, until moans escaped her helplessly again and again. Eager for more, she tried to find the buttons of his shirt, and when she couldn't she tugged at his collar, trying to push it out of the way.

He obliged her, sitting up quickly to shed it, then coming back so that bare skin touched bare skin in the most exquisite way.

"Ooh," she sighed contentedly, a contentment that didn't endure long as other, deeper needs clamored for attention. She writhed against him, trying to get closer, running her hands over the warm, smooth skin of his back.

"No hurry," he mumbled, to both of them it seemed to her, a reminder to enjoy every moment of this most wonderful of life's offerings.

But then her fingers felt something and she froze. A deep, puckered hole in his lower back. Awareness shoved her back to hard, cold reality. "What's this?" she asked in a tremulous whisper.

He stilled, and she knew the magic of the moment had snapped for him, too.

After a few beats, he rolled onto his side, carrying her

with him so that she was still securely tucked against him, her bare torso protected. Shielded. As if he sensed embarrassment might intrude.

"I was shot," he finally said.

Her hand found the scar again. "It was bad."

"Every gunshot is bad."

"No, I mean...there's a hole."

"That's the exit wound. They tend to be big and ugly, and take part of you with them."

"How bad is bad?"

"I lost a kidney."

"Oh, my God!"

"Hey," he said quietly. With one hand he began to tuck her shirt around her, covering her. Protecting her with her clothing as well as his body. Did he have any idea just how sensitive he was? How caring? She doubted it.

"Hey what?" she asked finally. "It's awful."

"I won't deny that. But I'm healthy. All I did was lose a spare. I'm lucky."

"Somehow I don't feel that way about it. How can you? Was that the only permanent damage?"

"I don't have a spleen anymore, either. But I'm still lucky. I should probably have died."

"Your partner did that?"

"Yeah."

She wrapped her arms around him as tightly as she could. As if she could squeeze away the pain and the memory. "And you had to kill him?" The true horror of it all finally dawned on her. His superficial explanation earlier hadn't really hit home. Now it did.

"Yeah." He shook his head, as if a fly were annoying him.

"Adrian. Adrian tell me."

"I did."

"No, I think you left things out. What exactly happened when you got to the house?"

"I told you, my partner was there. Talk about a shock. He was there, his gun was still in his hand, and he was standing over my informant. He'd just finished him off with a shot to the head. Why he didn't run when he heard me pulling up, I don't know. Maybe he thought I was someone else. Or maybe he honestly believed I'd just let him go."

"Let him go? Why? What do you mean?"

She felt his jaw clench, heard his teeth grind briefly.

"When he saw me, he sort of shrugged, as if it didn't matter. Then he said, 'Well, it had to be done. He's just scum. So we won't say anything about this, will we?'"

"Oh, God."

"Yeah, exactly. I guess he thought our partnership would mean more than the fact he'd killed a criminal. The thing was, it never meant more than that. It couldn't. And I knew immediately why he'd done it. He was dirty, covering his tracks by killing my informant. Did he really think that just because he was my partner I'd keep silent?"

"Maybe so," she said softly.

"All I know is, I told him to drop the gun, that he was under arrest. Instead he started walking toward the back door, away from me. He didn't think I'd stop him. So I pulled my weapon and fired at the wall beside him. That's when he turned and shot me. I was so full of adrenaline by then I hardly felt it."

He paused and she waited, knowing that he needed to gather himself. "Maybe he thought one shot would put me down and he'd be able to get away. Maybe he wanted to let me live. For damn sure that wasn't how we were trained to shoot. You fire three times. You make sure the perp is down and not getting back up. But he didn't."

"Odd."

"Yeah. But my training kicked in. I didn't shoot just once. I shot him three times, center mass."

She tried to squeeze him tighter, to let him know she was with him, because he seemed to have gone somewhere far away.

"He managed to stagger out the back door, but then he fell. By that time I knew I was in serious trouble, so I called for help. I don't know how I managed to remain conscious until they arrived, but I knew that I couldn't risk having him turn on me again, or that someone else would arrive and I'd be unprotected."

"I'm so, so sorry."

"Yeah. Me, too. Anyway, end of story. Help arrived before I passed out. I don't remember much after that. When I woke up again, I was out of surgery and they told me I'd recover. That I was lucky. I didn't feel lucky right then."

"No. I can understand that."

At last his gaze returned to hers. His eyes were dark with remembered pain. "He was my *partner*. For *five* years." As if that explained everything. And maybe it did.

Kerry tried to imagine that kind of betrayal, but all the times she'd felt betrayed paled by comparison. It wasn't like finding out a boyfriend was dating your best friend, too. This was far, far worse.

"I'm glad," she said, "that you're still alive."

"Sometimes I am, too." He sighed, and she loosened her hold on him just a bit. "That sounds ungrateful, doesn't it?"

"Well, I can see why you'd have a little trouble celebrating the whole thing."

He gave a short, mirthless laugh. "That's a fact. Anyway, when I recovered, and after some therapy, I realized I couldn't do the job anymore. I couldn't trust that way again, and that would make me a liability to a partner. I developed some paranoia."

"Understandably so."

"I also started doubting my own powers of observation. In retrospect, I sometimes think I should have caught on that something was going on with Barry before it came to that. Hindsight being twenty-twenty and all that. But the thing is, if I could miss that once, how could I be sure I wouldn't miss it again? So I'd never be able to work with a partner again. Or trust my judgment in quite the same way. I decided I'd be better off on my ranch, working with animals."

"Then you get dragged right back in."

"Well," he said with an evident attempt to lighten the

moment, "it didn't exactly happen right away. I've had two years to get over myself."

"Why do you think you need to get over yourself?"

His gaze grew quite serious. "Because people have to deal with even worse things than what happened to me."

"And that lessens what happened to you how?" Kerry shook her head. "I hate that attitude. Not that I think it does any good to drown in self-pity. Not that. But a trauma is a trauma, and comparing it to someone else's is as useful as comparing apples and airplanes. All each of us can do is handle our own life as best we can, and help those around us when we can. But it isn't helpful at all to belittle our own problems. You can't deal with a problem if you feel embarrassed about even having it."

"You might have a point there."

"Of course I do. I deal with teens all the time. Everything in their lives is magnified but it's wrong of an adult to minimize what they're experiencing. It's part of their growth curve, and if it seems like they're overdoing it, too bad. Because to *them* it's every bit as major as it feels. You can't help them at all if you dismiss what they're feeling, or if you try to minimize their problems. Perspective will come with experience, and *yours* will never work for *them*. They need to grow their own."

He nodded, one corner of his mouth curving upward.

"Anyway, don't dismiss your own experience and pain. Time may give you a different perspective, but you can't force it by comparing yourself to others."

"Thanks, Teach."

She looked at him suspiciously, but didn't see

anything in his face to suggest he was making fun of her. In the same moment, she became acutely aware of how they were lying, of how close they had come to a huge intimacy that she wasn't sure she was ready for.

She dropped her gaze, nearly closing her eyes. "I'm sorry," she said. "I can't."

"I know." He hugged her again, wanting to kiss her but not daring, holding her for several seconds before beginning to tug her shirt down again. "No apology needed, Kerry."

She nodded, grateful for his understanding, half-sorry she had ruined the moment by asking about his scar, and relieved that she had. Whether or not they ever made love, she sensed that it couldn't possibly be casual. There'd be a heavy risk for both of them, it wouldn't be something they could just walk away from as if nothing had ever happened.

She returned to her perch on the couch, unable to tear her gaze from the ripple of his muscles as he pulled on his shirt. She noticed he kept his back away from her, as if he didn't want her to actually see the scar she had touched.

He probably wanted to end that discussion, and she couldn't blame him for that. She had her own limits when it came to discussing the car accident and her near-death experience. One could easily cross the line between caring and prying.

"I'll make some hot chocolate," she said, the urge to do something overcoming her. Get back to normal. Get back to normal *now*. The only route to safety.

She rose and hurried from the room, seeking the

sanctuary of her favorite room in the house. As she pulled the mix from the cupboard, she heard Adrian step out the front door again to make his rounds. The instant she heard the door close behind him, it was as if the house emptied, leaving her alone and lonely. In that instant he took all sense of life and vibrancy with him.

The house felt as empty as a tomb.

Chapter 9

Lying on the couch with her head toward the fire and her feet toward the door, Kerry sought sleep and lost. Wide awake, she stared at the ceiling, watching the play of orange firelight and shadow on the ceiling.

She sensed that Adrian was awake, too, because he remained too still. Tossing on an air mattress could be noisy, but he didn't even roll over. If she paid attention, she could hear his measured breathing over the crackle of the fire. In fact, she could almost feel how intently he listened for any sound out of the normal.

But it wouldn't be a sound that warned them first. Somehow she knew that she would sense the approach of the killers before they tried to get in the house. If they came tonight.

That certainty surprised her, because her quirk or talent or whatever one wanted to call it could hardly be deemed reliable.

Yet there it was, that certainty. Comforting in a way, but discomforting at the same time.

Why had she even tuned in on this horror? It went so far beyond any past experience that all hope of understanding eluded her.

Unless...

The thought filled her veins with ice and she sat bolt upright.

"Kerry?" At once Adrian sat up, too, looking at her. "Did you hear something?"

"No. No. I just had a thought."

"What thought?"

"What if I know these guys?"

Everything seemed to hush, the fire and the wind both giving way in the face of some other dimension. Seconds stretched as nothing moved.

Then Adrian asked, "Why would you think that?"

"Because I've never experienced anything like this before." She turned her head on a stiff neck so that she could look at him directly. "I was wondering why I even picked up on this stuff. My past experiences with this...this ESP if you can call it that, were all about minor, inconsequential things that would affect me directly. This is a whole different scale. A whole different thing. And I didn't know the victims, so why would I pick up on it?"

He shook his head slightly, not in disagreement, but as if to say he had no answer.

"It just struck me that maybe I picked up on these crimes because I know the killers."

"I wish I could help you answer that."

"I can't answer it myself. Yet. But it would make sense. I mean, I'm not seeing other crimes, other murders. It's not that they haven't happened since the car crash, but I've never before gotten any information about them."

"So this stands out in more than one way."

"You could say that."

He scooted closer until he was sitting on the floor right beside the couch, facing her. "That's a really awful supposition."

"Tell me about it." She looked past him into the darkness beyond the range of the fire. "But it *feels* right if you know what I mean."

"Unfortunately, I do. The question is, how can we use the information?"

"But I don't know if it's accurate," she argued. "It was just an idea."

"For the sake of argument, let's assume you're correct. Does it tell us anything?"

She looked rueful. "It might if I didn't know most of the people in this county."

"True." He started to smile, but it never quite blossomed. "It's an interesting idea, though. One that might be worth pursuing."

"In what way?"

"Well, do you know anyone you suspect might be capable of something like this?"

"You know, that would be a funny question if this weren't so serious."

"I know. Ha ha."

"Exactly. What is it they always say? 'He was so quiet and kept to himself.'"

"Yeah, that's the line."

"Do you believe it?"

A small shake of his head. "I sometimes wonder. I mean, if you've got a guilty conscience or something to hide, yeah, you'd keep to yourself. But other people keep to themselves because they're introverts, or whatever. So it's hardly a diagnostic. Besides, all too often bad people don't see themselves as doing anything wrong. It's weird, but true. They always seem to have a good reason, at least from their perspective."

"Exactly." Sighing, she lay back against her pillow, resuming her contemplation of the dancing orange light on the ceiling. "I'm not going to sleep. But I doubt I'm going to get any answers. I could probably think about it all night and not come up with a likely suspect."

"So don't try to think about it. Sometimes things pop into our heads when we're not trying to get at them."

"Oh, *that'll* help," she said drily. "Don't think about it. Works every time."

He chuckled. "It's also possible you have no personal connection with any of this."

"I'd like to believe that." She frowned faintly, pondering. "That darkness is still out there."

He stiffened. "Getting closer?"

She shook her head. "It doesn't seem to be. But it's still there around the edges."

"Can you tell anything about it?"

"I'm not sure I want to. I'm thirty years old, Adrian, and I've been lucky enough never to have come face-to-face with real evil. I don't think I want that to change."

"But something has changed."

"Unfortunately." She closed her eyes, mentally feeling around. "Have you faced real evil? I don't mean just badness, but real *evil*."

"I know what you mean. I thought I had that day with Barry but you know, that wasn't evil, not the way you mean it. You mean it as something beyond ordinary human frailty, don't you?"

"Exactly." She rolled on her side so she could look at him. "I've always felt that evil resides within us, as part of our nature, that any of us is capable of terrible, terrible things. Sort of a feeling that who needs the devil when we've got us."

He nodded slowly. "I can see that. I've often felt that way. We can do truly great things, and then we can do truly terrible things."

"But..." She hesitated. "You ever see that picture of Charles Manson? The one where his eyes look so dark and empty? It was as if you see the abyss when you looked into them."

He nodded encouragingly.

"So when I go around making my blithe statements about evil, I have this niggling memory of Charles

Manson's eyes. There was something *in* there, and it wasn't Manson."

"You're talking about a different kind of evil."

"Exactly. An evil that's a force apart from us. That maybe takes us over and drives us to...something beyond ordinary human evil."

He nodded. "I know exactly what you mean."

"Have you ever encountered it?"

He hesitated. "Once. I interviewed a serial killer. Some of them are truly tormented people, but there are others who are so cold. Cold as the depths of hell."

She nodded. "And that's the feeling I'm getting, Adrian. Maybe that's why I sensed all this. There's something more to what's going on. Almost like possession."

She gave a nervous laugh. "I can't believe I'm talking like this."

"I won't tell, Teach," he said almost jokingly, but his expression remained deadly serious. "I know exactly what you're talking about. Don't dismiss it. I'd be the last person to claim I know the nature of true evil, but whatever its nature, it exists. And maybe that's what you're sensing."

"I think so. I don't even want to get close to it. It's hovering out there, and I feel like I want to pull the blankets up over my mind's eye so that it doesn't notice me. But it already has," she added, remembering the phone call. "So I guess playing ostrich would be stupid now, wouldn't it?" And as rationally as she was trying to discuss this, everything inside her seemed to be cringing away, seeking a bolt-hole to hide in.

"Well, it depends. Hiding physically could protect you. Hiding mentally could put you in danger."

"That's what I meant." She settled back against her pillow, and closed her eyes. "Always in the past I just got flashes of things. This is different. It's persistent."

"Maybe you need to stop fighting it then."

Her eyes snapped open. "I'm not fighting it."

"Are you sure? You don't want to know what it is. It scares you. I understand that, believe me. I was blind once, too, and I often think I refused to see what was right in front of me. Maybe this hovering darkness you sense is the same sort of thing. Something you'd prefer not to know because it could change everything."

She opened her mouth as if to argue, then closed it again. What if he was right? What if answers lay within her grasp but she was holding them at bay because she feared what she would learn? How could that serve anyone?

But by the same token, maybe whatever she was sensing was holding *itself* back, unwilling to be known.

That thought sent a shiver running down her spine; could she really attribute awareness to that darkness she sensed?

But she did, she realized. She had personified it, justifiably or not. Another shiver ran through her and she tugged the quilt up to her chin.

"What's wrong?" Adrian asked. "Do I need to throw another log on the fire?"

"I'm not cold. I'm scared."

He reached beneath the quilt and took her hand, giving it a reassuring squeeze. "You're not alone."

"I know." She squeezed his hand in reply, grateful for the warmth, grateful for the strength she felt there. "You really believe I'm sensing these things?"

He snorted. "I'd have to be an idiot not to. Think about it, Kerry. I wasn't a believer in psychic stuff before, but I am now. At least, I believe in *you*. I'm sorry you had to have these experiences, but you saved a life out there."

"And now you're having to sit up all night like a watchdog."

At that he winked. "Hey, sweetie, I'm better than any watchdog."

She nearly blushed, or maybe it was the heat from the fire. Handy excuse, anyway, for the warmth in her cheeks. And an equally handy moment of distraction. She would have bet he offered it deliberately. "You didn't just say that."

"Of course I did. And you know what? I can't be distracted by a hamburger thrown on the floor."

She couldn't help but laugh. "So you're a watchdog and I'm hamburger?"

He shook his head. "Oh no, Kerry. *You* distracted me."

"That does it." With her free hand, she pulled the covers over her head. A moment later he tugged them back down, smiling at her.

"No hiding from me. I'm your bodyguard, remember."

"That's what you call it?"

A full-throated laugh escaped him, then he leaned

closer, saying huskily, "Trust me, I'll guard your body even better when the time is right."

Any embarrassed impulse to laugh it off died as she looked into his eyes. Caught, she watched the firelight reflect there, but saw something even hotter behind the reflection. Every cell in her body turned instantly to warm honey, and she knew, just knew, that whatever her reservations, she needed to make love with this man.

Spending the rest of her life wondering would be the worst possible outcome, worse even than giving herself only to watch him walk away.

Never before had she felt this way about anyone. She almost pulled him toward her, determined to answer all her questions and needs right now.

But before the urge took over, she realized the timing couldn't be worse.

And in the instant it took to realize that, the darkness surged from the edges of her mind to front and center.

It enveloped her, smothering her, freezing her, holding her prisoner in her own mind. She heard a laugh, a voice she almost recognized, then a whisper, "You're next."

All of a sudden, so quickly it was terrifying, the darkness let go. She gasped for air, shuddering violently as if she had been buried in a snowbank, and vision returned.

"Oh, my God," she gasped. "Oh, my God!"

Adrian had her by the shoulders. "Kerry! Kerry, what happened? Are you okay?"

"No...no..."

He gathered her up then, pulling her into the warm shelter of his arms, tucking the comforter around her as if he could feel how cold she had become. Shivering violently, she pressed her face into his shoulder, seeking whatever heat she could find.

"What happened?" he asked again, working his fingers into her hair at the base of her skull, stroking soothingly.

"I don't know," she finally managed to whisper. "It was as if the darkness took over. I couldn't move, I was so, so cold, I couldn't even see. Oh, God, I felt invaded!" And soiled in some way. She wished crazily that she could toss her own mind into the washer.

He snuggled her even closer, sliding her from the couch to his lap as if he would surround her with himself. Little by little, feeling returned to her fingers and toes, making them sting as if she had been on the verge of frostbite.

Slowly she lifted her face to look at him. "It took all the heat from my body."

"It took the heat from the room right around you," he said grimly. "I felt it."

"God, what *is* it?"

"I don't know." His arms tightened even more. "I don't know what we're dealing with here anymore, Kerry. Honest to God, I don't. But I don't believe in possession. I don't believe disembodied spirits are hanging around the planet trying to do mischief. Do I believe in heaven? You bet I do. Do I believe that we survive after death? Absolutely. But I can't believe something disembodied took you over like that."

"Then what was it?" she demanded. "What happened to me? Damn it, Adrian, it wasn't natural!"

"I know that. I know that. But...but if you can psychically pick up on what these killers are doing, then why can't that same door work both ways?"

She bit her lip, trying to think. Even her brain seemed to have been laced with ice. "You mean like some kind of psychic telephone?"

"Maybe. Sort of. I guess what I'm saying is, if you can hear and see what they're hearing and seeing, maybe that's what just happened again. Only this time you picked up more strongly on their intentions, especially since they're directed at you, if that phone call wasn't just a prank. Maybe they're so focused on you that they broadcast those feelings."

"I'm not sure that makes me feel any better."

"It's better than positing a demon, don't you think?"

"Well, of course." The cold seeped away, and in its wake she felt utter exhaustion. Relaxing into his embrace, she stared into the fire and forced herself to think about what she had just experienced, much as she yearned to erase it completely. "I *did* hear a voice saying 'You're next.' And a laugh. And I felt there was something familiar about the laugh, but I can't place it."

"Well, don't worry about it. There are probably a lot of laughs that would sound familiar to you."

"I'm sure." A small sigh escaped her as she relaxed even more. "The mind-body connection is a strong one."

"Yes?" The single syllable encouraged her to talk as he began to rub her shoulder and stroke her arm.

"Well, yes. I'm sure you've heard how we can ramp up our immune systems merely by concentrating on it. Things like that."

"Some things, yes."

"Well, take just a small example. If you prick your finger with a pin, you feel it. But if you stimulate the same part of your brain, you'll feel that prick even though it hasn't happened. Or if we get scared, the body responds by pumping adrenaline. It's all of a piece. It's why, for example, curses can kill people who believe in them."

"Right." If he wondered where she was headed, he didn't press her to reach her destination quickly.

"So I was just thinking, the way I got cold and couldn't move or see, that may have been my brain's response to what I was sensing and it played out in my body."

"I see what you're getting at. That makes sense, actually."

"It makes more sense to me than that some kind of entity just walked into my mind and took over."

He nodded. "Me, too."

She sighed again, as if each sigh she managed to issue released more tension from her. "Whatever, I guess it doesn't matter. What I do know for sure now is that those killers are fully focused on getting at me."

"And that's when we'll get them."

She wished she could be as sure of that as he seemed.

Morning arrived covered in ice that coated every branch, every eave, every sidewalk and driveway. The grass sparkled as if it had been scattered with jewels and the ice in the trees acted like prisms, scattering light.

"A winter wonderland," Adrian remarked as he looked out the front window.

"It's amazing," Kerry agreed. "I don't think I've ever seen this before. Certainly not here."

With the sunrise came an easing of the night's tension, but Adrian thought the two of them looked like soldiers who'd been on watch all night in a battle zone. Or like hungover drunks after a binge. Red-eyed, rumpled and weary, neither of them looked fit to make it through the day.

Of similar minds, they'd already started perking a pot of strong coffee. Neither of them really had any energy for cooking, so Kerry pulled out some refrigerated cinnamon rolls and popped them in the oven.

"I'm not hungry," she remarked, "but maybe some calories will wake me up."

"Sleep will wake you up. After you eat, just go lie down and try to relax."

She gave him a wry smile. "Oh, sure. And you're going to stay awake?"

He couldn't resist her smile, and returned it. "Well, I wake easy. I know that for a fact."

"Yeah? How?"

"Hey, didn't I tell you about my experience with Uncle Sam's Misguided Children?"

"Who?"

"The marines. Four years, and I can sleep standing up with the best of them."

As he'd hoped, she laughed. "Why do I find that believable?"

"Because it's true. Ask any soldier. Being able to sleep anywhere, anytime, under any circumstances becomes a major talent. Pity those who can't learn."

She nodded. "You still look exhausted to me."

"I've been taking micronaps most of the night."

The oven timer dinged, and she pulled out the pan of rolls. The aroma alone made her mouth start watering. "So you were in the marines, and then you went into criminal investigations?"

"That's right. Can I put the frosting on those?"

"They need to cool for a little, first. Otherwise you'll need to eat the icing with a spoon from the bottom of the pan."

"That works, too."

She smiled again and he realized that somehow, some way, the entire atmosphere in this house had lightened again. As if the darkness had moved on. At least for now.

"You've done quite a bit in your life," she remarked.

"So have you."

"Well, I followed a pretty straight line."

He tilted his head to one side, studying her, thinking how beautiful she looked even after a sleepless night. "So did I. Macho meathead, that was me. Only I had to prove it. There were other ways I could pay for a college education, but I chose the manliest one I could find. The corps let me take correspondence courses, too, so when I got out, I had a lot of college under my belt already.

And my focus was always on criminal investigation. I always wanted to be a cop. Always."

She leaned against the counter and faced him. "And now? You're awfully young not to still have a dream."

He learned something about himself then. Something he thought he had lost was still there. "I'll find one," he said. And for the first time in two years, he believed it. "Maybe I'll just be the best damn gentleman rancher who never does a thing this county has seen."

She laughed again, the pretty, clear sound that made him think of small bells. "Somehow I don't think that will content you forever."

"Probably not," he admitted. "Now can I frost them?"

"Are you hungry or something?"

"I could eat a horse, if that didn't mean rustling one. Let me at them."

He shouldn't be feeling so good this morning, he thought as he drizzled the cream-cheese icing over the rolls. He should be uptight and worried and worn. Instead he had the craziest feeling that right now, just right now, everything was okay. That might change in an instant, but for these minutes, everything was fine. Better than fine.

Breakfast at the dinette in the kitchen turned into a good time. Coffee, rich rolls and good company. An unexpected reprieve in the series of bad days they'd been having. And so welcome after last night.

But Adrian couldn't fully lower his guard. A threat against Kerry lurked out there somewhere, and while part of him could take pleasure in their meal together, another part remained constantly watchful.

Nor did it soothe him to know the roads would probably remain impassible for several hours yet. The layer of ice out there was thick, and even if the day began to warm to more normal autumn temperatures, it would take time to thaw. Sand trucks had probably been out since before dawn, but the major roads, like the state highway, would be tended first.

Even as he had the thought, the ice claimed its due for the first time in town. The power flickered, then the house fell utterly silent. The heat had turned off, the light over the table blinked out. Even the hum of the refrigerator vanished.

"A tree must have fallen on the lines," he remarked. "Or at least I hope that's all it is."

Kerry nodded. "It may have, outside town."

"Keep the fire going," he said. "Use it to make us some coffee. I'm going to step outside and check around."

"Okay."

He pulled on his parka, checked his gun, then went out the back door, headed straight for where the power lines came into the house. Nothing there had been touched, which would indicate the problem lay elsewhere. A loud crack behind him startled him, and he whirled in time to see a branch tumble from a towering oak in front of the neighbor's house.

A lot of that had probably been happening around the town and county, of course. It was unlikely there was anything sinister going on. Still, edginess rode him like a goad. As if each passing minute only brought the threat to Kerry nearer.

A new deputy was parked out front, and he stopped by to chat with him. Except that him turned out to be her, Sara Ironheart. He had liked Sara from the first instant he clapped eyes on her, and she greeted him with a smile as she rolled down the window.

"I'm surprised you came into town," he said by way of greeting. "The roads must be hell."

"They are, but chains work well."

"How about Gideon and the kids?"

"They're fine without me. We lost power during the night, so they're camping in front of the wood stove and telling ghost stories. Oh, and drinking enough hot chocolate to sail a battleship."

Adrian laughed. "But there must have been someone closer to town to do shift."

Sara shook her head. "I've known Kerry most of my life, Adrian. I'm a lot older so we didn't hang out together or anything, but I know her. Like everyone around here, she's part of the extended family. I'll do my share, and I don't want any arguments about it."

"I'm not arguing. I'm actually glad to see you."

"I heard Cal was falling asleep last night."

Adrian winced. "I didn't want that to get around. He's young."

Sara smiled. "He confessed on his own. It's important to know the weaknesses of your fellow officers. You know that."

And boy, did he ever. He nodded, spoke with her a little longer, then returned to the house.

"Sara's on watch," he told Kerry.

"Good. I trust her."

"Me, too."

He found Kerry rinsing plates at the kitchen sink with cold water and stacking them. When she finished, she dried her hands on a towel. "I'm getting really cold," she remarked. "Back to the fireplace."

"You need a wood stove. Much more efficient."

"I know, but do you have any idea how expensive they are?"

"Actually, yes."

She looked rueful. "Every time I light a fire, I think about global warming. Some example I set for my students."

"Maybe you should build an igloo for the winter and wear sealskin."

"What, and kill all those seals just for clothes?"

He put his hands on his hips in mock irritation. "There's no satisfying you. You're ashamed not to be freezing to death because you're emitting carbon with your fireplace, but you won't kill a seal to make clothes."

"Think how much carbon I'd respire into the atmosphere with heavy breathing while I build the igloo."

"True."

"And I can't imagine how many months I'd have to chew the sealskin to make it soft enough to wear."

"You'd freeze by then."

"Most certainly. And wear my teeth to nubs. So I still need a fire, I guess."

"Damn, but it looks that way."

He knew he wore a cockeyed grin, but he was fairly certain it wasn't any more cockeyed than hers.

"So what's the solution?" she asked.

"We could follow the geese south."

"Only if we walk. Anything else will require planting a forest to balance the emissions."

"Hmmm. That's a long walk, and right now I don't think we'd get past the edge of town."

"So we're stuck for the winter."

"At least."

"Which means," she said, "that I'm heading for the living room to take advantage of the emissions I'm currently responsible for."

"Makes sense to me. I mean, if you're going to burn the wood, you might as well be warm."

Still smiling, she headed that way with him on her heels. The living room was pleasantly warm, not overheated as it would have been had she put on too much wood. They sat side by side on the couch, silent now. He supposed they were both remembering the waiting game they played.

For many years he had noted how the male deer would seem to fade away come hunting season. You'd still see the does, but the bucks, either with a biological rhythm born from years of being hunted, or alerted by the first gunshots of the season, seemed to vanish from the earth.

Hence the deer feeders so many hunters relied on now, something he thought utterly unsportsmanlike.

But thinking about how the bucks faded into the deepest woods when they were hunted made him wonder if they were making a big mistake by keeping Kerry at her house. Still, in a place like this where gossip could pass to the farthest end of the county between dawn and dusk, he wasn't sure anywhere else would be safe, either.

And there was another thing, an unspoken thing, something he suspected Kerry already knew.

She had become bait.

Chapter 10

The phone rang, startling them both. Kerry hadn't switched over to the cordless variety—the only reason she still had service. Paling slightly, she watched as Adrian answered it. A moment later she relaxed as she realized he was talking to Gage.

"Yeah," he said, "everything's okay here. Except for the power outage. How bad is it?" He listened. "Okay. No, we've got enough wood to get by and there seems to be enough food for a day or two. How about the victim in the hospital?"

When at last he hung up the phone, he turned to look at Kerry. "Well, the outage is bad, and we can probably expect not to have power in this part of town until early tomorrow, if then."

"And the woman in the hospital?"

"She's talking, but basically she didn't see a thing except her friend getting shot. As soon as she felt the bullet in her own arm, she took off away from the sound of the shot."

Kerry nodded. "All she could do."

"Yeah. Thank God she did. But apparently it was her husband and her friend's husband who were the first victims. The two guys were rock hounds who'd take trips two, maybe three, times a year looking for unusual specimens. Apparently one of them taught at the university in Laramie and the other taught high school science."

"That poor woman!"

He nodded grimly. "Right now I'm feeling like I'm on a shrinking ice floe."

The reference to their earlier joking held no humor. That was exactly what it felt like, Kerry thought. That or a tightening noose.

"I'm sorry," he said abruptly. "If I could, I'd take you as far away as I could get you."

"I know, Adrian." She believed he would. "But that's not going to happen."

"Not this morning at any rate."

"Not at all." She shook her head a little and looked down at her hands. "If they're stupid enough to come after me, it's the best chance you'll have to get them. I read enough to know that finding a killer who isn't connected in any way to a victim can be extremely difficult."

"Well, harder than if it's the husband."

The attempt at humor fell utterly flat in the too-quiet house.

She gave him a wan smile. "I could use a little ESP right now."

"Let me know if you get any. Because right now I'm willing to act on anything you pick up."

She nodded. "It seems to me that having a deputy parked right out front is more of a hindrance than a help."

He drew a sharp breath and she watched the frown crease his face. "Kerry, we have to be sensible about this. I'm not going to dangle you out there like a judas goat."

"But that's what I am. Or what I should be. We've got to stop these guys, Adrian. And at the moment I seem to be the only connection you have."

"No."

She leaned back against the cushions, letting her head loll and closing her eyes. "I'm not afraid of dying."

"Has it occurred to you that I might be afraid of losing you?"

She couldn't bring herself to open her eyes. Her heart seemed to stop mid-beat, and the breath sailed out of her. "Adrian..."

"Just don't argue with me, Kerry," he said urgently. "Just don't argue. I know you're bait. I know you have been since that phone call. But none of us, me most especially, is willing to risk you recklessly. You've got to understand that. You've got to."

At that she opened her eyes and looked at him, reading the urgency in his face, the deep concern, even the flicker of fear. She understood that it would kill him to lose someone he was protecting again. She also understood that if he was ever to trust again, she had to do what he said. Unfortunately for them both, there was a life in the balance, and it might not be hers.

"I won't do anything stupid." That was as far as she could promise.

"Did I say you would? But don't ask me to send the deputy away. There are two of them, you said. There's only one of me. That's not enough coverage."

Almost as if to reinforce his message, he swept her up off the couch and carried her back to her bedroom. Any objection she might have framed vanished in the wonder of his concern. In the strange security of being in the arms of a man who could carry her so easily. Why should that make her feel safe?

But it did, and more, it yanked her out of the frightening present to another place, a warm place where the sun could shine again and she could forget all this horror. Yes, she'd said she didn't want to make love. Yes, she'd meant it then. But not anymore.

Turning her face, she buried it in his shoulder. "Adrian...I...want you..."

"Shh," he said gently. "I want it, too. And God help me, I need you now."

He placed her on her bed, and she watched through heavily lidded eyes as he stripped away his clothes. God, he was beautiful, she thought hazily. So beautiful. And somehow she sensed that his willingness to toss away his clothes was a huge emotional step for him. That he was saying he had begun to trust her.

That thought added an emotional warmth to the physical heat that seemed to come out of nowhere and light every nerve ending with a flame.

Whatever he was trying to tell her, she was more than ready to listen.

Kneeling beside her on the bed, Adrian began to undress Kerry, taking his time to drop kisses on each newly exposed area. From her throat down, he worked his way slowly, trying to draw out this moment even as his own body throbbed insistently.

Somewhere in the mix of heady desire, he was aware of the risk he was taking, a risk for both of them. But he had to convince her not to take a foolish risk. He had to convince her how much it mattered to him that nothing harm her.

Issues of trust hardly seemed to matter when compared to the enormity of the threat she faced, and the worse threat she was prepared to face out of some crazy idealistic notion that she mattered less than stopping these killers.

He could think of no other way to persuade her that she mattered just as much as any other possible victim, not less just because she knew she was in the line of fire.

And this seemed to be the only way he could speak of his deep fears for her, of his need for her, of all the things that had become paramount for him over the last few days.

There weren't words for this, not even for a poet. What he felt was so deep and so elemental he wasn't sure he understood it himself.

But he could talk with his hands, and his body, could try to make her feel all that he was feeling.

And that's exactly what he did. He devoted himself to her pleasure. He wanted to give her an experience that would make her want to live, an experience that reminded her that even though death didn't scare her, there was something to *live* for.

He teased her nipples with his tongue, enjoying the way she began to moan softly, the way she began to move, at first gentle lifts of her hips. When her hands reached for him, he shifted away, denying her only because he wanted to draw this out, and because he wanted to drive her mad with longing.

Her skin was soft, smooth, living satin. As he teased her breasts with his mouth, his hand began to wander, finding every little place that could make her shiver. When he at last reached the pelt between her legs he found it soft, too, and a chuckle almost escaped him when she arched upward, seeking more than teasing touches from his hand.

Not yet. Not yet.

His own excitement kept him on the precipice, too, the throbbing of his body strengthening until he dimly realized that never, ever, had he felt desire this strong. And he was determined to make her feel the same.

Kerry's whole world settled between her legs. Every touch he gave her only added to the deep, pulsing ache she felt. Her entire body responded, lifting toward him, writhing in harmony to the heavy pulsing deep inside.

Each time she reached for him, he seemed to slip away, but never did he leave her.

She hardly knew the deep groans she heard were her own. Somehow the physical sensations in her body transcended the physical, became something more, something greater.

Hunger, yes. But a divine hunger, man for woman, lover for lover.

At last she could bear no more of his teasing and she turned herself toward him, seizing him, finding one of his nipples with her own mouth, nipping gently with her teeth until a groan rumbled upward from his depths.

There was a horrible moment when he stopped. "No condom."

"No!" She tried to grab her bedside drawer. There were a few there, kept for a dream that hadn't happened until this moment, probably way too old, but nothing was going to stop her now.

He helped her grab one, then she tore the packet with her teeth and rolled the latex onto his staff, watching the way he grimaced with pure pleasure at her touch.

Moments later he was over her, then sliding into her, into a place so long-empty she had forgotten how glorious it felt to be filled.

He whispered her name, then moved. His thrusts were deep, demanding. His body shook with the power of his need, and his need fed hers until she rose to a place where pleasure and pain became the same thing, a need so strong it actually hurt.

And then...and then...

She found a different kind of heaven. Moments later he shuddered and collapsed on her.

She never wanted to let go.

They cuddled together on the bed, covered by the quilt, entwined tightly. If either of them could speak, neither of them wanted to for a very long time. To hold and be held, to feel skin on skin. Did life offer anything better?

But eventually the sound of an icicle dropping from the eave outside her bedroom jolted them both back to reality.

He looked at her, cradled her face in his hands, and kissed her soundly. "We need to get dressed. This was dangerous."

She assumed he meant because someone wanted to kill her, but she also suspected there were other ways the hour just past could be dangerous to both of them. She didn't want to think about that now.

Rising, her entire body telling her that it wanted to remain in the warm bed with Adrian, she pulled on her clothes. By the time she finished, Adrian had already gone to prowl the house.

To escape her, she thought sadly. To pull back from an intimacy he didn't want. Could she blame him?

No, but she felt as if her heart were ripping open anyway.

She stepped into her flannel-lined moccasins and slowly followed him back to the real world. He was in the living room, reheating the coffee by the fire. "Want a cup?"

Between one second and the next, something in her shifted. A different connection snapped into place.

With deep certainty, she started speaking, though she couldn't have identified the source of the knowledge, only her certainty. "The killers are stalkers. They'll wait out the ice. They'll wait for an opportunity to get at me, Adrian. And they'll get one. But if we don't catch them soon, someone else is going to die first. The compulsion...won't let them stop."

"Compulsion?"

"It's a game. But it's more than a game. One of them is compelled like an addict. The other one is getting there. And someone else will die. A woman. A woman with a baby."

At that she gripped his forearm and leaned toward him. "A woman with a baby. We have to stop them, Adrian."

"Then tell me where they are. But for God's sake don't ask me to stake you out in the open and hope I can move quick enough from behind some blind."

But she had gone to another place, one farther away, slipping there without consciously realizing it. "They already have her," she said. "She lives with one of them. This weather...this weather is causing problems. He needs his fix, but he can't get out to hunt. The hunger grows in him, every time he looks at her. He's already thinking about how her eyes will look as her life fades...."

When she returned to self-awareness, Adrian was already on the phone, relaying the information to Gage. He looked at her. "How old is the baby?"

She felt strangely disconnected, and there seemed to be a fog or a mist in her mind, concealing things, making it hard to think. But then, "Just a few months."

Adrian relayed the information. She hardly heard him wind up the conversation, really noticing only when he drew her into his arms.

"They're going to look," he said, almost rocking her. "They're going to look. There aren't that many babies that young in this county."

"They've got to save her."

"If they can they will." There was no mistaking the steel in his voice. He'd made up his mind about something, but she didn't want to ask. All she wanted to do was let him hold her close and keep the demons at bay.

And yet the vision would not leave.

The woman took the baby. She felt the eyes of the older man fixing on her in a way that deeply frightened her. She didn't know for certain what her boyfriend and that man meant when they talked about their hunting, but she had a terrifying idea they weren't comparing elk to deer.

So while they played cards in the front room with the curtains pulled against the blinding brightness of the light that splintered off all the ice, she slipped into the baby's room and wrapped the infant in every piece of warm clothing and receiving blanket she could find. She stuffed the diaper bag with necessities and the little bit of money she had saved from her limited household budget.

Then, nearly tiptoeing, she eased into the mudroom, closing the door silently behind her. The baby slept, thank God, and remained sleeping as she hastily pulled on her own cold-weather clothes. Better clothes were available these days, but he wouldn't get them for her, so she made do with her father's insulated work pants and her mother's old wool coat, and a knitted wool scarf and mittens she had made herself.

Then, with only the merest creak of hinges, she stepped outside with her baby and closed the door tightly.

There was only one direction she could take that would not bring her in sight of the windows of the front room. Even though the curtains were drawn, she feared one of them might look out.

She headed straight back for the woods, knowing her trail would be plain to see unless the sun melted the ice swiftly.

But she knew in her bones that remaining here exposed her to even more danger. She knew those men were able trackers who could probably follow her to the ends of the earth.

But she also knew some secrets, secrets she had never shared with anyone. If she could make it to the creek, she could cover her tracks and make her way to a cave that was so well hidden she had found it only by falling into it as a child.

She could hide there.

The only question was how long she could survive in the cold.

Kerry snapped back to herself, shaking from a cold and a horror that penetrated to her very bones.

"Oh, God. There's such little time!"

Chapter 11

Around midday, the temperatures began a sharp rise, melting the ice swiftly. The county began to move again, and even from the vantage point of her house on a narrow side street, Kerry could tell that people had begun to hurry around to deal with their regular Saturday chores and errands.

It would have been nice to do the same, but she didn't even ask Adrian if they could. Much as cabin fever had begun to irritate her, some other sense kept her nailed indoors.

It was, she thought, as if she were waiting for something.

Her imagination, perhaps, ignited by the threatening phone call? Possibly.

But something was about to happen, of that she felt increasing certainty.

The phone rang, and once again Adrian took the call. "Okay," he said. "Good."

When he hung up, he turned to Kerry. "They've pretty much talked to all the new mothers."

"And?"

"There's one missing. Her husband's missing, too, and some guy who lived with them."

"That's them!" How she knew, she could not say. "Did you get a name?"

He shook his head. "So now we know who we're looking for, I guess. But whether the woman and her baby are still alive, no one knows."

Kerry closed her eyes, seeking a flash of perception, suddenly longing for the visions she had never wanted to begin with. Nothing answered her, not one damn wisp of intuition. "I don't know," she said finally.

"No reason you should." His voice suggested that he wanted to comfort her, but it also suggested something else.

Fear.

The killers were out of pocket, assuming the absent men were the right ones. They might even now be killing the woman with the baby. Or they might be coming for Kerry. She knew what he was thinking without asking.

Because she was thinking the same thing.

"I don't like this," he said finally. "Most of the deputies are out looking for these guys and the woman with a baby. Hardly anybody's here in town."

"I'm exposed."

"That's what I was getting at, yes."

"It's okay."

"No, it's not!" He snapped the words and she took a step backward, her eyes widening.

"Sorry," he said after a moment during which he visibly gathered himself. "But we've got a couple of killers running around the county, they've threatened you, and my backup is that kid in the car out there."

"Kid?"

"The one who fell asleep at the wheel last night. He replaced Sarah."

"Cal? He's an okay kid. I taught him."

"I don't trust him. He fell asleep on the job."

"It's daytime now."

"Yeah. Sure."

He started pacing, and she had the feeling of a huge wolf on the prowl. He was as tired of being locked up as she was. But was there an alternative?

That's when it struck her. "Let's go."

"Go?" He froze, staring at her with disbelief. "Go where?"

"Let's go looking for them."

"You're out of your mind."

"No, I'm not." She leaned forward earnestly. "Think about it, Adrian. They're out there somewhere and they know where I live. I'll be safer on the move than sitting in this house."

He shook his head sharply, but it wasn't exactly a

denial. After a moment he said, "Do you think you might get some sense...if we're out on the road?"

"I don't know," she admitted. "But sitting here is making me feel like a target in a carnival booth. And you're right. We have too little backup here, not with everyone out looking for a woman with a baby. It's worth a try. It has to be. I can't just sit here and do nothing."

He was thinking about it. She could see it in his eyes. He hesitated for at least a full minute. Then he wagged his finger at her. "You sit right here. I'm gonna go talk to Cal, then I'm gonna call Gage. After I talk to them, I'll decide just how harebrained this is."

"Of course it's harebrained. But it could work."

She could tell he didn't like the idea at all. But he didn't say any more. He simply left her in the kitchen and headed out front.

Sitting there by herself, she wondered if she'd lost her mind, or if this was as good an idea as she thought when she had formulated it.

Because there was no mistaking that she was offering to put herself in a noose.

Gage proved remarkably sanguine about the whole idea. He stopped by in answer to Adrian's call.

"Sure," he said. "It's a good idea."

Adrian frowned. "She's already a target, and I'm supposed to expose her all over the county?"

"Moving targets are harder to hit."

"My thinking exactly," Kerry said. Although in fact

she was beginning to doubt her own sanity. She was actually volunteering for this?

Now Adrian frowned at her. "You're not afraid of dying. Do you know how much that terrifies me?"

Gage ran his fingers through his hair, the gesture of a man who has just realized he may have put his foot in it. Before he could reconsider, Kerry spoke.

"Look Adrian, if it's any comfort, the idea scares me, too. I don't *want* to die, and I promise I won't behave rashly. But this has to *end*. Quickly. I can't stay in this house forever, and I certainly don't want to keep having visions of people being murdered. Do you know what kind of hell that is? Plus, I couldn't live with myself if someone else dies because I sat here and did nothing except hide. You should be the last person I need to explain that to."

Gage looked at Adrian, wisely keeping his mouth shut.

"I know. I know," Adrian said finally, repeating himself as if reassuring himself in some way. "It's just that..." He appeared unable to find the words he wanted.

Kerry had no idea what possessed her then, but she said something brutally true. "It's not me you don't trust. It's yourself."

If it were possible, Gage seemed to blend with the wall.

Adrian gave a sharp shake of his head. "You sure don't pull any punches, Kerry."

"Should I?"

Adrian looked away, seemed to stare at something beyond the walls that surrounded them. "You'll have to wear the armor," he said finally. "And promise me you won't do one damn thing without my permission."

"I'll try not to."

He glared. *"Promise."*

"I can't. I never make promises when I'm not sure what might happen."

"God!"

"I can send Cal with you," Gage offered. "It'll be some added protection."

"No," both Kerry and Adrian said at once, rounding on him.

"Cal is useless," Adrian said. "He'd probably just get in the way. He's too new, and I don't need to be looking out for anyone else."

Kerry added her own objection. "We're just going to be driving around. Didn't we agree a moving target is harder to hit? They won't know where to look for me. All I want is to get a fix on where *they* are."

Somehow, however, Gage seemed to think the matter was settled. "You've got your hands full, Adrian. I'll get you both fresh radios. They're in my car."

He departed through the front door, leaving Adrian and Kerry to stare at each other.

"I'm sorry, Adrian," she said quietly. "But I *have* to do this."

After a couple of seconds he nodded. "I get it," he said. "Believe me, I understand. But I don't like it."

"Neither do I, honestly."

The bubble of tension between them began to deflate,

and the space between them no longer felt like an emotional no-man's-land.

"It's that woman and baby," Kerry said quietly. "I can't ignore them."

"No. I can't, either. I just wish there was another way."

"Maybe there will be. Gage must have people searching all around that house."

"Of course he does. He told me as much. Which is why I'm having trouble with the idea that you have to get involved."

"Would you have found that wounded woman if I hadn't been there?"

"No, but that's not the point."

"Isn't it?"

"It's not like you can be a hundred percent sure you'll pick up anything."

"But I have to at least try."

Apparently he could understand that, because he loosed a sigh, shook his head and then turned to get her body armor. Gage returned then with two radios. "They haven't found a thing out at that ranch where the woman and baby live. But they're still looking. If either of you gets any other ideas, let me know."

Despite the possibility that he might be driving Kerry into the lion's den, Adrian headed straight for the ranch where the searchers were already looking. It seemed like the best place to start.

Between them on the seat was a thermos of coffee.

Behind him on the gun rack were his two favorite shotguns.

"You ever use a shotgun?" he asked Kerry.

"Of course. I live in Wyoming."

"You take one, then, if we get out of the truck."

"Are they loaded?"

"Not at the moment. Ammo is in the glove box."

"Okay. Which one do you prefer?"

He glanced at her. "You take the Mossberg," he said finally. "It auto loads six rounds."

She nodded. "I've used one."

He took what solace he could from that and the fact that you didn't have to be a sharpshooter to hit your target with a shotgun. Whether she could actually bring herself to use it against a human target remained to be seen.

"I've got low-recoil mag rounds for it," he went on, wanting her to have any little bit of info that might prepare her. "But you've got to be ready to use it, Kerry. Otherwise you might as well carry a club."

"I hope I don't have to find out if I can."

"Me, too." To his everlasting sorrow, he *knew* he could fire at a human being. He'd have vastly preferred to never learn that about himself. He hoped like hell Kerry could escape that discovery.

They were still on the county road, climbing steadily toward the mountains, within five miles of the ranch they sought when Kerry said, "Pull over."

He didn't bother to question, just edged over onto the muddy shoulder, keeping two wheels on pavement.

When they stopped, he quietly waited for her to speak again while keeping an eye out.

Trees dotted the landscape here, and they clustered as if outlining a stream bed that ran toward the mountains. Out here a lot of the ice still remained in patches of shadow.

After a couple of minutes, Kerry shook her head. "Nothing," she said. "Let's keep going."

He shifted into drive and pulled them back onto the road with only a brief wheel spin in the mud. "Did you get something?"

"I thought maybe. But it was just a fleeting thing."

"Maybe you shouldn't try. I mean, everything else you've gotten has been pretty much when you weren't expecting it."

"True." She settled a little more comfortably in the seat. "Have you ever noticed how uncomfortable these vests are?"

"Every time I wear one. They've gotten a little better over the years, but not a whole lot."

"I guess that's basically irrelevant when you think about *why* you're wearing one."

"Unless it gets really hot, yeah."

"Don't turn off at the ranch."

The command was abrupt, and Adrian glanced her way. Her face seemed to have frozen. Questions weighted the tip of his tongue, but he swallowed them, not wanting to disturb whatever sense she was getting.

Just a few weeks ago, he would have believed he was on a wild-goose chase. No more. At this point he was willing to credit her instincts as much as his own. After all, who was to say where a hunch came from?

Sure, the argument said they were based on experience, some idea or feeling arising from the subconscious assemblage of knowledge gleaned over time, but when he watched Kerry do this thing of hers, he wasn't at all sure that was the whole story.

How many times had he acted on a hunch he couldn't explain even to himself? Plenty. Maybe the only difference between him and Kerry was that he could point to his experience as a police officer to justify his hunches, while she had nothing to point to except the feeling itself.

Wherever they came from, her intuitions had made a believer out of him.

A sheriff's car with flashers on was parked at the entrance to the ranch. The Crooked M. Kerry struggled to remember who owned the place. The deputy motioned them to stop, so Adrian braked. Almost at once he was recognized.

"Hey, Adrian," said Fred Wehrung. "Do you need to go up to the house? I'll need to call ahead."

"No," Adrian said. "We're on our own goose chase."

Fred half smiled. "Hope you do better than us."

"Is there any indication these folks left the ranch?"

"Other than them being gone, you mean?" Fred shook his head. "All vehicles registered to them are still there. It's got us all wondering if they might be vics, too."

"No," said Kerry. "The men are the perps. The woman is a victim. Or will be soon if we don't find her."

Fred hesitated, looking at her, but apparently he'd heard about her visions, too, because he nodded. "You be careful then. Do you want any help?"

"Not yet," Adrian said, feeling reluctance all the way to his bones. A posse would have been a nice thing right now. But it might also interfere with the very thing he and Kerry were out here trying to do.

"Stay out of trouble," Fred said, waving them on.

Adrian hit the accelerator, and the mountains came a little closer. "Stay out of trouble?" he repeated. "If we were going to stay out of trouble, we'd be on our way to Laramie. Or Gillette, or Casper, or Denver, or..."

Kerry gave a little laugh that didn't sound as if she really meant it. "Maybe we can do that later."

"Yeah. Keep saying things like that and I might hold you to them."

She glanced at him. "Do you think I wouldn't want you to?"

He turned and met her gaze as a deep pothole shook them. "Ask me that again when this is over."

Kerry sank back into her seat and wondered how to take that. Yes, she'd realized when they made love that might be as far as he would ever go, but then to say he might hold her to her offer to take her away, and back off just as quickly...

Oh, what did it matter? she asked herself irritably. Her whole life had turned on its head since her first vision—gee, was that only a couple of days ago? It seemed like an eternity now. Which was probably a measure of just how much had happened and how much it had changed her. A lifetime, it seemed, had compressed itself into a handful of days.

Nothing looked the same anymore, not the countryside around her, or the looming mountains, or even her self-image. Did she even know herself anymore?

The last time she had felt so shaken in her world had been after the accident. Now here she was again, shedding an old self the way a snake shed its skin. Growing pains? Or something else.

She didn't know.

All she could be certain of right now was that something was pulling at her, tugging her forward, making her do things she wouldn't have done even one short week ago. And part of that tug came directly from the man beside her.

She hated to think that Adrian would most likely return to his own life after this was over, and put her as firmly in his past as he had put other things. As everyone had to put things.

Because life seemed to move only in one direction, and right now they were hurtling blindly along some road, carried on a stream of forces that felt beyond their control.

In fact, if she allowed herself to really think about it, she should tell him she was nuts, that he was nuts to listen to her, that her ESP must be evidence of insanity and following her in this proved *his* insanity and...

This whole line of thought seemed to spring more from a sudden panic than from reason, she realized. Although reason had little to do with the visions she'd had, reason demanded she not ignore what had already proved itself.

"Stop!"

The command erupted from her lips before it reached her brain. Adrian jammed on the brakes, throwing them both hard against their seat belts.

"What the—"

"Just stop," she said, her voice suddenly reedy. "Just stop. I don't know..."

Her voice trailed off and she began to look around, feeling frightened, yet knowing at the same time that it was not her own fear she felt.

"Someone's scared," she said. "Terrified."

"Nearby?"

"I don't know. Just wait. Please. Wait."

He fell silent.

She looked around, her gaze bouncing from tree to bush to fence post and back as if she couldn't find exactly what she sought. Finally she reached for the doorhandle and started to open it.

Adrian grabbed her arm, his grip viselike. "Don't," he said.

"I have to get out. I have to."

"Then just wait a minute. Let me check around first."

The compulsion that gripped her at that instant didn't want to yield to caution or reason, but she forced herself to nod. Her hand never loosened its grip on the door handle, though.

Adrian set the parking brake, then climbed out. She watched impatiently as he walked around the truck, taking stock of their surroundings. It took him entirely too long, and impatience built in her, growing as rapidly as the fear she sensed. Apparently nothing worried him because he finally came to her door and opened it.

"Okay," he said.

She accepted his help as she stepped down. As soon as her feet his the ground, however, the feeling dissipated.

"Damn it!"

"What?"

She looked up at him, feeling as if her entire face had grown pinched. "It's gone. Just like that it's gone!"

He exhaled heavily. "Okay. Okay. Look, let's just stay right here for a few minutes, have a little of that coffee we brought along. If it comes back, it comes back. If not, we'll drive a little farther."

His plan made as much sense as any at that point. He helped her back into the truck and poured them both a steaming cup of coffee in the mugs they'd brought along. Kerry cradled hers in both hands, as if to stave off a chill, but the chill she felt lodged deeper inside, in a place no coffee could reach.

"I hope they didn't find her," she said.

"God!" He didn't have to say any more.

"But I don't think it's that," she said slowly. "It was more like when you lose the signal on the radio."

"And considering you don't have a dial you can adjust, I guess we'll just have to wait until it drifts back."

"That's a good way of putting it. Unfortunately, there's more at stake here than hearing a particular song."

"Quit pressuring yourself, Kerry. My God, you've already done the impossible. I get the feeling this is something you can't force."

"I wish it were."

"So sure of that?" He looked perfectly serious.

"What do you mean?"

He half shrugged, as if he wasn't quite sure himself, then said, "Maybe I just have this feeling that life is easier to bear when we *don't* have extra-normal knowledge."

"Paranormal, you mean."

"If you say so, Teach. But here's the thing: After what I've seen, I don't want to call it paranormal anymore. That sounds like hokum."

"Well, I seem to have a case of hokum."

He gave her a wry smile. "Not in the least. If I thought that, I wouldn't be chasing all over the county right now." Reaching out, he clasped her hand and squeezed it.

She squeezed back, grateful for his support and strength. "I had a friend in junior high school who used to have precognitive dreams. Only they weren't about little things, but about important things. Major disaster stuff, like plane crashes and earthquakes. After a while, there was no way to call it coincidence."

"That's scary."

"Well, I can't say I got scared. But I sure understood when she told me she wanted it to stop. She said she couldn't do anything to prevent it, so why know about it in advance? She said it was useless and upsetting, and she didn't want it anymore."

He nodded. "I can see that."

"The thing is, once she made up her mind that it had to stop, it stopped."

She could see him turning that over in his mind. "Interesting."

"I thought so, too. But I'll tell you, I want this to stop. Once we finish this, I want it to stop."

His hold on her hand tightened. "I understand."

"The thing is... Well, you'll probably think I'm crazy."

"If there's one thing I'm sure of, it's that you're not crazy."

"Sometimes I feel like it."

"Who doesn't?" The question carried just a hit of humor. "But what were you going to say?"

She sighed and stared down into her coffee mug while clinging to him with her other hand. "Sometimes I believe in destiny. Which is not to say I don't believe in free will. Of course I do. I don't believe that everything in life is planned for us. It's just that sometimes I think certain things are meant to be. That we're slated to have certain experiences. Destined, if you will."

"I can buy that. Some things have almost a feeling of inevitability to them. A sense that no matter what, we're going to arrive at a certain point in time and face certain issues."

"Exactly! But then when that moment or event comes, we still have to make choices."

"Yeah. The outcome isn't destined. It isn't fixed."

She looked at him. "That's it. So it's like I was meant to have these visions for some reason, that a lot of things led me here. There was no escaping it. The only question is what I do about it."

He nodded. "You could choose to go to Denver."

"Yes. That's exactly what I'm getting at. So maybe, for some reason, I *had* to experience this, but it's what I do about it that counts."

She looked out the car window, across small fields hemmed by a thickening forest. "I felt that way about the car accident, too. Maybe it was just a form of survivor guilt, I don't know. But I'd get this feeling that there was a reason. Maybe this was it."

"I can't begin to answer that, Kerry. All I can tell you is that I definitely *do not* believe that life is a random series of events without meaning. But even so, every moment of our lives we make choices. It's the choices that matter."

She nodded then took a deep drink of her coffee. "That's kind of how I feel, too. This whole thing has made me think hard about it. I mean, right after my friends died in that accident, these kinds of questions preoccupied me for a long time. But then, you know how it is. You can't operate that way all the time. Eventually you sink back into the comfort of familiarity and sort of letting life wash over you. No long-term perspective, no soul-searching questions."

"We'd go nuts if we didn't do that. Or we'd have to retreat to a mountain hermitage. Most of the time we just have to be in the moment."

At that she gave him a wry glance. "How many of us actually live in the moment, Adrian? We're always thinking about what's ahead, what's just behind. The moment is mostly that elusive point from where we look forward or back."

"True."

"Ironic, isn't it? If you think about it, we're everywhere but *here*."

A quiet laugh escaped him. "You hit that nail on the head, Kerry."

"You saw my book collection. I read too much. But there's a common theme in a lot of stuff, the theme that we need to be *in* the moment if we want to be happy, not living in a future that hasn't happened yet, or a past that's done."

"Nice philosophy, except that we need to store up our acorns against the winter."

"Ah, but remember the lilies of the field..."

He smiled. "Neither do they sow nor do they reap... Yeah, I remember that. I've always loved that verse."

"Easier said than done." She looked out the window again, suddenly feeling an uncomfortable prickle at the base of her skull. "I'm tuning in. Can you drive a little farther?"

"Sure." He balanced his mug on the dash and started them down the road again.

The mug jolted and Kerry reached out, grabbing it and holding it. "I think you'd prefer the coffee in your stomach, rather than your lap."

"That's usually the way."

She didn't answer him, but instead tried to let the feeling grow in her, that sense that she knew something she couldn't quite put her finger on.

"I need to get a newer truck," he muttered. "One with better suspension and some cup holders."

She only vaguely heard him. Something was rising out of the depths of her unconscious, or whatever place those paranormal impressions came from. She tried to just let it happen, but couldn't quite prevent herself from trying to hurry it along. She said a quiet little prayer that they'd find this woman and her baby before it was too late. Just that. She wouldn't ask for any more than that.

"Stop."

Chapter 12

Adrian hit the brake and looked at her. She was still staring out the side window. "Here," she said. "Here. They're out there. All of them. They're hunting her and the baby."

"God."

"We've got to go. Here. Now."

He didn't argue. He set the brake and turned off the ignition. After radioing in to tell Gage they were stopped and where they were getting out, he gave Kerry a long look. When he climbed out, this time he reached for the shotguns. Kerry sat on the seat, seeming to have forgotten she held the coffee mugs, still staring toward a line of trees.

Reaching across her, he pulled open the glove box

and took out the ammunition. He loaded both shotguns, then stuffed his pockets with more.

Then, guns in hand, he came around to the passenger side and looked at her. "You should stay here," he said.

"You'll never find her." She put the mugs on the dash and opened the door. Sliding to the ground, she sought steady footing in the soggy ground.

He passed her the Mossberg. "Can you reload?"

She nodded.

He reached back into the cab and took out a couple more handfuls of mag shells, filling her parka pockets. Then he stuffed the ammo boxes back in the glove box and locked the truck. From the bed he grabbed a heavy backpack and slipped it on. Camping and survival stuff—in case. It was the kind of stuff a wise person always carried in the winter around here and there weren't a whole lot of daylight hours left.

"Okay. Get your gloves on, zip up and make sure you're ready."

She nodded, following his instructions.

"You stay behind me," he cautioned. "Tell me where to go, but keep a low profile, okay?"

"All right." She indicated some trees with a movement of her chin. "That way."

"Try to stay in my tracks. You'll be less likely to stumble."

The morning's sunshine had begun to give way to a gray layer of clouds, flattening the world with diffuse light. Not the best conditions.

He had to lift barbed wire out of the way. Gone were

the days of wide-open spaces, except in parks and national forests. Everything belonged to someone now, and everyone had fenced his piece of the world.

She slipped through without any trouble and he followed her with only slightly more difficulty. Then, with her right behind him he began slogging toward the trees she'd indicated.

He glanced back once and saw that she carried the shotgun carefully, muzzle pointed away and down, strap arranged to properly brace the gun if she fired. So he didn't have to worry about that. She *did* know what she was doing.

The morning's thaw hadn't been helpful at all. Ground that was usually hard had grown spongy, and only the browned grasses kept them from sinking. Still, it was a bit fatiguing, like walking in sand.

Ten minutes later they reached the trees and he paused, turning to look at Kerry. She appeared to be listening, so he didn't say anything, simply waited. As long as they had only her impressions to guide them, this was going to be slow.

"Somewhere," she whispered, as if to herself, then closed her eyes.

While she checked in to the parallel universe where things were revealed to her, he kept watch, scanning the surrounding woods with a practiced eye. Funny, he'd never thought he'd need most of his marine training again, but right now it was coming to the fore as seldom before. Patrol in enemy territory, that's what this felt like. Two killers on the loose, God knew where.

"That way," she said finally, indicating a path deeper into the woods. "She's near water."

"I think there's a stream back there."

Kerry nodded. "Do you have a map? It might help."

He turned his back toward her. "You see that little pocket on the bottom of my pack? Map and compass."

She zipped it open and retrieved the waterproofed map and the compass, then passed both to him. He opened the map, studying it for a few moments before pointing. "This is where we are. And there's a creek back there."

She leaned over, looking at the map. "How can you be sure?"

"This was the easy stuff when I was a marine."

"Oh, I almost forgot you were in the corps." That seemed to settle her mind. "After you."

Taking his direction from the map, he used the compass to keep them on course in woods that grew darker and thicker the farther they walked. At least as the woods thickened, the undergrowth diminished, providing fewer obstacles. And in the woods the ground had not thawed as much.

Until they started to climb, and rock outcroppings began to force them to divert. Adrian moved ahead confidently, though, because even without a compass he knew he could bring them to the stream. The compass just made it quicker and surer.

Water from melting ice dripped from high branches, adding an almost musical sound of "plop-plop" to the forest. Apart from a few squirrels, the wildlife had gone into hiding. Still, he knew they were being watched. Their passage wouldn't go unnoticed by nature.

Then, halting him in his tracks, a wolf coalesced out of the shadows, seeming to grow from nothing. Kerry stopped behind him and looked around him. "Oh," she breathed.

Golden eyes regarded them steadily. The wolf kept one paw lifted as if about to dart away. His coloring reminded Adrian of a husky, although the animal looked scruffier than any pet. He still hadn't finished his autumn shedding, and appeared almost moth-eaten.

Moth-eaten but powerful, the apex predator in these woods and mountains. Even bears could be taken down by hungry wolf packs.

But if there was a pack, it remained out of sight. A judgment was taking place, and Adrian waited patiently for the decision.

At last the wolf seemed satisfied, and melted back into the shadows whence he came.

"Wow," Kerry breathed. "I've never seen one in the wild before."

"Few people do. They're pretty shy."

"He didn't seem shy."

"He's probably the alpha. Has to protect the pack. I think we've been granted safe passage."

"That was so cool."

Adrian nodded, agreeing with her. But he felt his own rising sense of urgency and began to lead the way toward the stream again.

Then, seeming to come from everywhere around them,

the howls of the pack rose, an eerie harmony that could make a half dozen wolves sound like so many more. Adrian stopped again, and this time Kerry gripped his arm.

"Is that a threat?" she asked.

"I don't think so," he said after a moment. "It's probably an announcement that this is their territory. I don't think they'd do that if they wanted to attack."

"I hope you're right."

He glanced at her. "Wolf attacks on people are so rare I can't even tell you. We're more likely to get trouble from a bear."

"You *had* to say that."

"I was speaking in general. This time of year, most of the bears are in their dens."

"Asleep."

"Not quite. They can still rouse to protect themselves, but if we don't threaten them, they'd prefer to keep hibernating."

"Do we need to be quiet?"

"Why do you ask?"

"Well, I was wondering, if wolves are so shy, why do people think they're killers?"

He paused and faced her. "Myth. Legend. The rare attack on the weak and the sick when the climate was harsh. You get hungry enough, you'll attack whatever's available. Even if it's the species you domesticated into friends."

"Wolves aren't domesticated," she said.

"I didn't mean them. The wolves domesticated us, or that's what a lot of biologists think now. We fed them.

They kept watch at night while we slept. By and large, that relationship works fine. But there are exceptions...."

"Why does every good thing have exceptions?" she asked.

"Not every good thing," Adrian said with a smile. "There were no exceptions last night. And from here on out, I think we'd better be as quiet as possible. We're not far from the stream, and if those guys are out hunting, I'd rather they not hear us from miles away."

She nodded just as the wolves let out another eerie song.

Adrian leaned down to her ear. "We might not be alone."

She realized he wasn't referring to the wolves.

At once the back of her neck prickled. She gave a quick nod of understanding, and shifted the shotgun to a readier position.

It occurred to her that if the wolves were warning invaders from their territory, the warning might not be directed only at them. Now, she thought, would be a good time for a little intuition, except that she had none.

Of course. Remembering her friend who had died, she wondered, *What good is it if it isn't there when you need it?*

But that was the whole problem with the psychic thing. If it were as reliable as the other senses, it wouldn't be paranormal, would it? And people would be more inclined to believe it.

In fact, the whole world would be different, so she might as well stop complaining. Right now they had a woman and infant to find, and all she could do was pray that they'd be in time.

And keep moving. They had to keep moving.

The howls sounded again, but from a different place. The pack was on the move, too. Somewhere out there, they had found another invader. The chill that crept down Kerry's spine now had nothing to do with the weather.

When the woods fell silent again as if even the trees had frozen to acknowledge the wolves' claim of primacy, Kerry for the first time thought she heard the sound of running water. She eased forward until she walked beside Adrian and cocked her head toward the sound.

He nodded, then motioned her to step behind him again. She understood that he didn't want her to trip, but she also feared they just made a better target this way.

She whispered, "Shouldn't we spread out?"

"If you were trained. You're not."

She couldn't argue with that. What did she know about stalking killers in the woods? Not a damn thing.

The soft ground muffled the sounds of their movement, and Kerry found herself making every effort not to even let her parka rustle. The nylon, so good at keeping her warm, wanted to announce her every movement.

Ten minutes later, they were almost at the stream. The sound of running water filled the air now. Adrian motioned her to hunker down with him behind a boulder.

"Okay," he said in a whisper just loud enough to be heard over the rushing water, "we have to make some decisions here. You said the woman and the child are near water?"

She nodded, remembering her earlier impression.

"It's likely, if the killers know her and are stalking her, that they're moving along the stream, too."

"The wolves were howling to the east." She pointed.

He nodded. "The question is whether they were howling at the woman, at the killers, or at a fox. God knows."

Kerry looked around, as if she might see answers hanging from the trees like Christmas ornaments. But of course she saw nothing but tree trunks, scrub and an endless carpet of pine needles and leaves.

"Great," she muttered. "What good does it do for us to be here if we don't know what to do next?"

"That's the thing," he said. "You're going to stay behind this boulder while I go look."

"No!"

"Shh! Stay here. I need you to cover me while I go look to see if the river bank is disturbed."

At that she subsided. At least he wasn't leaving her behind out of some misguided notion of protecting her.

"I can do that," she said. "I used to be a decent shot."

"Then I don't have to tell you not to aim that thing too close to me."

"Of course not."

"If it comes to that, I'll have to protect myself. The spread on that load isn't huge, but it's enough to lay two people out if they're close."

"I know." She did. "My dad used to take me for target practice."

"Not hunting?"

"Are you kidding? You think I'd want to kill some inoffensive deer?"

A smile cracked his somber expression. "Why doesn't that surprise me?"

"My dad hunted elk and moose. He stopped hunting deer."

"Why?"

"Because I got really, really nasty about it."

"But what makes deer different from moose or elk?"

She could tell only part of his attention was on what she was saying. His eyes kept scanning their surroundings as if he had built-in radar.

"They can be mean. Besides, we had to eat."

At that she got his full attention, but only briefly. "You'll have to tell me about that some time. But right now—"

She touched his arm, silencing him. "I feel them."

"Who?"

She closed her eyes, letting the faintest whisper of intuition grow, nurturing it without trying to hurry it, for fear she might banish it. Adrian waited, but she sensed his impatience.

Time. Time. Time was growing short. They were getting closer. They...they...

Which they? The woman? The killers?

"They're almost here," she whispered. "Almost."

"Who?"

A different voice emerged from the woods. "Well, what have we here?"

Kerry's eyes snapped open as she felt Adrian tense beside her. She turned her head and saw a man holding a rifle pointed at them. Him. A bearded older man in camouflage.

As she felt Adrian start to move, she touched his thigh. "Behind us, too," she whispered.

"God."

"Why don't you just put down those guns," the man said, the barrel of his rifle never wavering.

Adrian tried playing dumb. "Why? Can't a man hunt anymore?"

"How stupid do you think I am?" The man turned his head and spat on the ground. "That teacher there, she reads minds. I heard all about it."

Ice seemed to encase Kerry's heart. But she knew what she had to do.

Slowly, she put the Mossberg down. Then, despite Adrian's objection, she rose until she stood, facing the man, her hands held out to show they were empty. "I don't read minds."

"Sure you do," the guy said. "I heard all about it. Even the sheriff is listening to you."

"Who told you that?"

"None of your beeswax. Now get away from that guy so I can keep an eye on you."

Kerry started to obey, but Adrian gripped her ankle, stopping her.

Adrian spoke. "You sound crazy, you know that? Mind reading? If she could do that, I'd be playing the lottery."

A branch cracked behind them, telling them where the other man was.

"I told you, woman, move away from him."

"He won't let me."

"Oh fer Pete's sake..." The man leveled his rifle at Adrian, but just as he did so, Adrian yanked on Kerry's ankle. Loss of balance sent her to the forest floor in an eyeblink. Barely did she register that she had fallen on her shotgun when shots rang out. She heard the buzz as a bullet flew by her and the *thwack* as it hit the boulder. Another bullet came from a different direction but she couldn't tell where it went. Only that the cracks of fired guns were coming from two directions.

Rolling slightly, she grabbed the Mossberg and released the safety. Pressing the stock against her shoulder while lying on her back, she raised her head to try to find the second shooter.

Even as she did so, there was another crack of gunfire. This time it was Adrian. He'd drawn his pistol from wherever he had concealed it and fired past her toward the guy who had first accosted him.

Then she saw the second man, and something took over. In an instant she sat up and aimed the Mossberg at the man, a younger version of the first. His eyes widened, and before she could pull her trigger, he dropped his own rifle.

"Don't," he said. "Don't."

She kept the shotgun trained on him.

"Watch him," Adrian said.

She glanced at him, then gasped. There was blood on his sleeve, and his face had gone white.

"Adrian..."

"Watch him, damn it! I've got to take care of the other one."

She obeyed, realizing she had no other choice. "Don't move," she said to the young man. Then her heart slammed as she recognized him. "My God, you're Tom Martinez."

He nodded, keeping his hands up.

"Why in the world are you involved in this?"

Adrian pushed himself to his feet and walked toward the other man, pistol still pointed at him.

"He's only wounded," Adrian said. "Keep your eye on Tom."

Kerry couldn't have taken her eyes off of him. He'd been her student only six years ago. A bright one. She couldn't imagine what had led him down this path.

A *snick* followed by a ratcheting sound told her Adrian was putting cuffs on the other man. Another half minute passed, then Adrian walked past her toward Tom.

"Facedown on the ground, hands behind your head," Adrian told him.

Tom didn't even resist. He did as he was told while Adrian fixed nylon flexi-cuffs at his wrists and ankles.

With both men bound, Adrian returned to sit beside Kerry, sliding down the rock as if feeling weakened. "I'm counting on you," he said.

Then he pulled out his radio and called for backup and medical aid. As soon as he got an affirmative response to the location he provided, he leaned forward.

"Get the first-aid kit out of the pack."

He still held his pistol, so she put the Mossberg aside

and did as asked. The first-aid kit was right on top, and she pulled it out.

Adrian used one hand to unzip his jacket. "Feel around in there. Top of my right shoulder. Stuff gauze into it on both sides."

She obeyed, pulling his jacket open. She had to bite her lip when she saw how heavily he was bleeding, but urgency drove her as she stuffed the wound with gauze, then reached for a second roll and wrapped it, tightly as she could, trying to make a pressure bandage.

"Thanks." For a few seconds his head fell back against the boulder. "I'll be okay. It's not as bad as it looks, Kerry. Now take care of him." He nodded toward the older man.

"No."

"What?"

"I don't care if he dies after what he did. But I'm not going close to him."

Adrian, some of his color returning, looked her right in the eye. "You're better than that."

"Wanna bet?"

But she grabbed the first-aid kit anyway and stomped over to the wounded man. Adrian had bound him hand and foot, too, but his wound didn't look that bad. At least it wasn't bleeding much. Ignoring the groans of pain that came in response to her ministrations, she put gauze around his thigh, and tightened it with a sharp jerk.

"There," she said. "More mercy than you gave your victims."

His eyes opened, and the coldness in them was

enough to make her step back. Another second of that
stare sent her hurrying back to Adrian's side. He already
looked almost back to normal.

"I don't believe in possession," she said when she
returned to Adrian. "But whatever is in that man's eyes,
it isn't human."

"Yes, Kerry, it is. It's just the worst part of us."

She shuddered. "I'd rather believe in demons."

The radio crackled to life, and the subject was
dropped as Adrian guided the deputies toward them.
Twenty minutes later, the first pair came crashing
through the woods, their hurry making them sound like
a Mongol horde.

Next to Adrian, Kerry thought, they were the best
sight she'd ever seen.

Chapter 13

Once the paramedics had finished giving Adrian a temporary patch job on his shoulder, he refused to be taken to the hospital.

"We've got to find that woman and her child."

Arguments that there were now plenty of other people to aid in the search didn't deter him. Questioning of the two suspects had revealed nothing. Despite having shot at Adrian and Kerry, they insisted they'd been hunting. Tom Martinez claimed to have no idea of where his wife and child had gone. "Probably to visit a friend," he had said sullenly.

When the two men had been taken away, Adrian walked down to the stream bank and squatted. The water ran between stony banks, offering nothing in the way of tracks.

"But would a woman with a baby have walked on the rocks?" he mused.

Kerry squatted beside him. "Yes, if she didn't want to leave a trail."

He nodded. Behind them, Gage and his deputies were planning the search. They decided the bulk of them would head downstream toward the ranch.

"That's wrong," Kerry said. Leaning forward, she dipped her hand in the icy running water. At once something electric seemed to zap her.

"She walked in the water."

Adrian turned to look at her. "What?"

"Her feet are wet. She's shivering."

Kerry herself started shivering, as if she had merged with the woman in some way. "Dark. Cold. Musty. Grace..."

"Grace?"

Adrian stood up and called to Gage. "Who are we looking for?"

"Maria Martinez."

"Not Grace?"

Kerry turned in time to see Gage freeze. "The baby is Grace."

Kerry straightened and looked upstream. Then, without a word, she started walking that way. The rocks made it difficult, so without another thought, she stepped into the stream. The years of erosion had made the stream bed relatively smooth, covered in egg-sized rounded pebbles and smaller. Easier than the bank where the rocks were far bigger and less stable.

"Kerry!"

Adrian called after her, but she ignored him. She had to keep moving. Upstream. Farther. Until she reached the boulder that parted the waters. Already she could see it in her mind's eye.

Splashing behind her told her she was being followed. Her feet rapidly grew numb from the cold water, but each step seemed to bring them back to life long enough to feel burning pain.

At some level she became aware that deputies were following her, moving alongside the stream, clambering over rocks and around vegetation. Adrian was right behind her, and soon he was there to steady her with a hand on her arm.

He didn't say another word, just let her lead.

Tired. So tired. Cold. Grace. Keep her close and warm. Don't sleep.

Her eyelids felt heavy, but they weren't her eyelids. They were Maria's. Stay awake!

She didn't know if the thought was her own or Maria's and she was past caring. All she could do was hurry her step.

She'd been keeping her head down, watching her step, focusing on the inner voice. Suddenly she looked up and there was the huge boulder, taller than a tall man, dividing the waters.

Without a thought, she turned to the right and began to scramble up the bank.

"Kerry?"

Adrian was right behind her.

"Shh."

He fell silent except for the sounds he made climbing behind her. Here the slope was steep, leveling out only when they stood high above the stream. A few deputies, watching them, began to cross the stream toward them.

"Here," Kerry said. "Somewhere right around here."

Adrian turned slowly, scanning the rough, tumbled terrain.

"Maria!" Kerry called out. "Maria, we've taken Tom and Henry into custody. I'm here to help you and Grace!"

Everyone froze, listening. In the distance the wolves howled a mournful sound.

"Maria! You need to get warm. Grace can't take as much of the cold as you can!"

Silence. Then a faint voice responded. "Here."

Kerry couldn't tell exactly where it came from, but Adrian seemed to.

At once he began walking toward a rise, a tumble of boulders covered with brush. "Maria," he called gently. "Maria, I'm with the sheriff. We want to help you."

"Here," came the thin voice again.

Adrian dropped to his knees and began to pull rocks away. An instant later, Kerry joined him, her frozen hands oblivious to cuts and scrapes. Rock after rock tumbled down the slope as they were pulled free.

Then a small, dark cavern appeared. Kerry didn't hesitate, but crawled right inside.

"She's here!" she shouted the words as she crawled the last two feet to the woman and child. "It's okay, sweetie," she said to Maria. "It's okay. We're going to take you and the baby to the hospital, okay? And Tom and Henry have been arrested. Can you move?"

Maria's only answer was to hold out the bundle she clutched.

Kerry took it, and realized it was the baby. Pulling the blanket a little to one side, she saw the infant's face. Nearly white with cold, but still breathing.

At once she eased back through the opening. Adrian started to reach for the child, but Kerry shook her head. "Help Maria."

He at once crawled into the opening. Kerry struggled to open her parka with one hand, and tucked the bundled child inside, close to her body's heat. Her own feet were frozen, her hands little better, but as soon as she unzipped her parka she felt the heat rise from her torso and touch her chin. Once she was sure the child could breathe all right, she zipped it into the parka with her.

Then, slowly, she eased her way down the slope toward the approaching deputies.

"The EMTs are coming," one of them assured her.

"Good. This baby is nearly frozen."

But she herself was little better, and finally the cold took its toll on her.

Slowly she collapsed to the ground, unable to take another step.

Sitting in a heap, she began to rock back and forth, arms wrapped around herself and the infant.

Right now, she couldn't even feel relief. Maybe that

would come later, but at this moment she felt as close to dead as she had after the car accident.

Only this time she didn't see the light.

Noise filled the emergency room. From a cubicle some distance away, Henry could be heard cursing as a doctor examined his wound. Grace's thin cry intertwined with the nasty words erupting from behind a curtain.

Kerry lay on a pad that circulated warm water from her neck to her feet. A couple of thick blankets covered her, too, but she still shivered. It might have been lingering hypothermia for which they were treating her, or it might have been a reaction to events. She couldn't tell. Nor did it matter, really.

All that mattered was that there would be no more killing. Right now her heart felt light, as if she had shed a burden.

But all she wanted was to go back to a normal life. No more visions, no more fear, no more ugliness. There was, she thought, nothing more beautiful than ordinary life.

A nurse, a former student of hers, popped in to peek at her feet. "Looking good," Cheryl said. "I think you'll be out of here soon with all your parts."

"That would be nice. How are Grace and Maria doing?"

"You know I can't tell you that. Of course, I was more worried about your feet..."

Then Cheryl vanished, pulling the curtain behind her.

Sideways message received, Kerry thought. The warmth cocooning her made her body feel sleepy, but her mind still raced a mile a minute trying to absorb all that had happened. It would probably do that for days. It was the way of the mind to endlessly replay important events until some kind of organization and absorption had been achieved. At least that's what they had told her after the accident.

Closing her eyes, she let the images and feelings roll like an instant replay of the past few days. At some point she must have dozed off, because the next thing she knew, a warm, strong hand clasped hers.

Her eyes popped open and she found Adrian sitting on the edge of the bed beside her.

"Welcome back, sleepy head."

Her gaze flew to his shoulder. Beneath his torn and bloodied shirt, she saw a professional bandaging job. A sling bore the weight of his arm. Instantly she filled with relief and warmth, a different kind of warmth than the one wrapping around her frozen body. He was okay, and he was here.

"How's your shoulder?" she asked immediately.

"The guy was using a .22. Through and through, muscle tear, no major damage. I guess he was trying to avoid hitting me in the vest. Either that or he's a lousy shot."

"Thank God! What if he'd gone for your head?"

"Didn't you ever learn not to shoot for the smallest part of the body?"

Something in the way he said it made her giggle. The giggle had an edginess to it, as if the response wasn't relaxed. Too early for that, she thought.

"Your feet?" he asked her.

"Cheryl says I get to go home with all parts attached."

"That's great news!" He smiled and squeezed her hand. "Hey, Teach, it's over. You saved the day."

She shook her head. "I didn't really do anything."

"What?" He frowned. "I seem to remember you doing quite a bit."

"The visions just came. It's not like I made them happen."

"But you stuck with them. That couldn't have been easy. Then out there in the woods, you were incredible, Kerry. Incredible. I've never had a better partner."

The words warmed her all the way to her toes, even more than the heating pad beneath her. A flush crept into her cheeks, but she didn't know how to respond.

He astonished her by leaning forward and kissing her lightly on the lips. "What say we blow this joint?"

"Can we?"

"Cheryl told me to come get you."

A smile filled Kerry's face. "But Grace and Maria are okay? Nobody will tell me."

"Nobody will tell me, either, so before I came to see you, I popped in on their cubicle. Mother and child are doing very well. Scared and alone, but at least they're healthy."

"For now I guess that's all we can ask."

"No, we can ask a whole lot more. We can ask for justice. And we will," he said, taking her hand as he eased himself off the bed. "But justice takes time. For now, I'm going to ask for something else. Take me home, Kerry. Please. And stay with me."

Home had never felt so good. Despite the fact that Adrian was the wounded one, he insisted on taking care of Kerry. Pillows propped her comfortably on the sofa, a blanket covered her legs, a fire crackled in the fireplace. Darkness had fallen beyond the windows, but it was no longer a darkness that held threat.

Adrian pulled the easy chair up beside the couch so they could sit side by side, then disappeared for about twenty minutes. When he returned, it was with hot cocoa and a package of chocolate chip cookies. He put everything on the coffee table, then took a plate and arranged cookies around her mug on it.

The gesture made her smile as he handed it to her.

"I feel like a princess."

"You always should." His own smile was warm as he sat in the easy chair with his own cocoa and a stack of cookies he hadn't bothered to arrange.

"I'm glad it's over," she said, looking at her plate mostly because she was afraid to look at him. It was over, all right. And in a little while, he'd walk out of her house to return to his own home, and that would be that.

"So am I. But mostly I'm glad you're safe and there's no need to worry about those guys anymore."

"Does anyone know why they were doing it?"

Forgetting his wounded shoulder, he shrugged, then winced. "From what Gage said, they were treating it like a game. More exciting than stalking deer. Although how you can think it more exciting to walk up on unsuspecting campers and shoot them beats me."

"It wasn't the stalking," she said after a moment. "It was worse."

"Worse?"

"It was the kill. The thrill of killing a human being."

He set his mug down and twisted to look at her. "Another vision?"

"Not exactly." She shook her head and remembered. "That man's eyes. Henry, right? It wasn't about the hunting, it was about the killing. I felt it when I looked at him. Anybody can kill an animal. Not everyone can kill a human being in cold blood."

"Not everyone can kill an animal, either, but I see what you're driving at." He sighed. "Worse, I think you may be right."

"I just wish I could understand how Tom got himself involved. He seemed like a nice, ordinary kid when he was my student."

"Maybe he was, once. He wouldn't be the first person to be led astray by a powerful personality. It happens all too often. Then, once you get someone like Tom started on the path, they begin to justify it to themselves. I've seen it before, although not in a case quite like this."

"I suppose. I remember reading some psychological studies in college and coming away amazed at just how suggestible people are. It doesn't take much."

"That's one of the reasons we try to keep witnesses separated until we have their statements. Otherwise one of them could convince a dozen others that they all saw an atomic bomb explosion when all they heard was a backfire."

One corner of her mouth lifted. "A little extreme, maybe?"

"Unfortunately not. A person who assumes a position of authority can convince people to do things they'd never otherwise do. Or even change what they remember."

"I've heard that if you have ten witnesses to a crime, you're apt to get ten different stories."

"Something like that. Hell, they won't even agree on what color shirt the perp was wearing. If you start with that and someone appears to be certain that it was a white T-shirt, then pretty soon everyone else will be sure it was a white T-shirt despite the fact the perp was wearing a purple sweatshirt. It's amazing."

"Well, I guess we'll learn all about it when they come to trial."

"Or from Gage. Don't forget, I have inside sources."

"So did they," she said, shaking her head. "When we were about to leave the hospital, didn't Gage say Tom fingered Cal as the one who'd been telling him about the investigation?"

"Yeah," he said, nodding. "Gage doesn't know what to do about that. Cal and Tom were friends back in school. Cal had no idea Tom was involved. He was just sounding off to be impressive. Half the department wants to throw the book at him. The other half just wants him fired."

"I'm sure Gage will make the right call," she said. She was too tired to worry about Cal's future right now. And too worried about what was going to happen with the man who sat beside her. She was just beginning to realize that if he walked away, she might seriously want to die.

He grew serious. "How do you feel? I don't mean physically. The emotional strain has been awful for you."

"Not only for me. You were charged with protecting me. I can't imagine how rough that was for you after what happened before."

"Well..." He managed a crooked smile. "I seem to have found a partner I can trust."

Her breath caught in her throat and her eyes locked with his. The heat she saw there awoke an instant yearning in her. "You hardly know me."

"Guess what, Teach. You learn to know the important things real fast under circumstances like this. You were willing to do anything to save Maria and Grace, and you don't even know them. Do you know what it was like to follow you up that stream, knowing you were in danger of losing your feet? Or of dying from hypothermia? But you kept right on, and you didn't stop until you had that baby safe. I saw you collapse. Kerry, you were pushing forward on sheer will even before we started climbing the bank."

She colored. "What else could I do?"

"Exactly." He leaned toward her until their faces were inches apart. "I saw what you did when those men had us at gunpoint. Damn it, you were trying to protect *me*."

She shook her head. "You can't know that. Heck, I don't even remember what I was thinking just then."

"I could tell by what you did. And I can tell you right

now, I'd trust you with my life. I hope you feel the same way about me."

"How could I not? Adrian, you've been protecting me for days."

"Trying to, at any rate."

She lifted a hand and cupped his cheek. "You're a remarkable man."

He took her cocoa and cookies, placing them on the coffee table. Then he leaned in and kissed her with all the passion of a thirsty man who has found water.

"We need time," he said huskily. "I want to get to know you a lot better. I want you to know me better. But I can tell you right now, Kerry, I love you. And I don't think anything is going to change that."

"I might have annoying habits." The protest was weak, silly and an attempt to buy a few seconds as her heart lurched into her throat with a kind of fearful excitement. She wanted to believe him, but with what they'd been through, how could he be certain he wasn't just feeling some kind of aftereffect?

"You can have any annoying habit you want," he said throatily. "There's not a single thing you can do that will change my mind. I know the stuff you're made of. I trust you. And I love you."

A single tear squeezed out of her to tremble on her eyelashes. A single tear of happiness. "I love you, too," she replied, and the undeniable truth of those words filled her with an emotion that went far beyond any words. The strength of the feeling nearly squeezed the breath from her.

He kissed her again, long and deep, promises and the seeds of promises in his touch.

"I won't rush you," he said, looking deep into her eyes. "I promise I won't rush you. But I'm going to marry you."

Another feeling came to her, one of those she'd been having for days now. Her quirk. But this time the feeling was good.

"Yes, you are," she answered. "You most certainly are."

Because she *knew*. And she saw the smile on his face as he realized where her certainty came from.

Visions of destiny.

* * * * *

*Celebrate 60 years of pure
reading pleasure with Harlequin®!*

*Step back in time and enjoy a sneak preview
of an exciting anthology from
Harlequin® Historical with*
THE DIAMONDS OF WELBOURNE MANOR

This compelling anthology features three stories
about the outrageous Fitzmanning sisters. Meet
Annalise, who is never at a loss for words… But
that can change with an unexpected encounter in
the forest.

*Available May 2009
from Harlequin® Historical.*

"I'm the illegitimate daughter of notoriously scandalous parents, Mr. Milford. Candidates for my hand are unlikely to be lining up at the gates."

"Don't be so quick to discount your charms, my dear. Or the charm of your substantial dowry. Or even your brothers' influence. There are as many reasons to marry as there are marriages."

Annalise snorted. "Oh, yes. Perhaps I shall marry for dynastic reasons, or perhaps for property or influence. After all, a loveless, practical marriage worked out so well for my mother."

"Well, you've routed me on that one. I can think of no suitable rejoinder." Ned rose to his feet and extended his hand. "And since that is the case, let me be the first to wish you a long and happy spinsterhood."

Her mouth gaped open. And then she laughed.

And he froze.

This was the first time, Ned realized. The first time he'd seen her eyes light up and her mouth curl. The first time he'd witnessed her features melded together in glorious accord to produce exquisite beauty.

Unbelievable what a change came over her face. Unheard of what effect her throaty, rasping laughter had on his body. It pounded a beat upon his ear, quickly taken up by his pulse. It echoed through him, finally residing in his stirring nether regions.

So easily she did it, awakened these sensations within him—without any apparent effort at all. And she had called him potentially dangerous? Clearly the intelligent thing for him to do would be to steer clear, to leave her to the tender ministrations of Lord Peter Blackthorne.

"You were right." She smiled up at him as she took his hand and climbed to her feet. "I do feel better."

Ah, well. When had he ever chosen the intelligent path?

He did not relinquish her hand. He used it to pull her in, close enough that he could feel the warmth of her. "At the risk of repeating Lord Peter's mistake and anticipating too much—may I ask if you'll be my partner in battledore tomorrow?"

Her smiled dimmed. Her breath came a little faster. His own had gone shallow, as if he'd just run a race—and lost. He ran his gaze over the appealing lift of her brow and the curious angle of her chin. His index finger twitched.

"I should like that," she said.

His finger trembled again and he lifted it, traced the pink and tender shell of her ear, the unique sweep of her jaw. Her pulse leaped beneath her skin, triggering his own. Slowly he tilted her chin up, waiting for her to object, to step back, to slap his hand away.

She did none of those eminently sensible things. Which left him free to do the entirely impractical thing.

Baby soft, the skin of her lips. Her whole body trembled when he touched her there.

He leaned in. Her eyes closed, even as she stood straight against him, strung as tight as a bow. He pressed his mouth to hers. It was a soft kiss, sweet and chaste. And yet he was hot and hard and as ready as he'd ever been in his life.

She drew back a little. Sighed. Their breath mingled a moment before she slowly backed away.

"Oh," she breathed. Her dark eyes were full of wonder and something that looked like fear. He took a step toward her, but she only shook her head. His outstretched hand fell to his side as she turned to disappear into the wood. This was the first time, Ned realized. The first time, since he'd come to the house party at Welbourne Manor, that he'd seen her eyes light up.

* * * * *

*Follow Ned and Annalise's story
in May 2009 in
THE DIAMONDS OF WELBOURNE MANOR
Available May 2009
from Harlequin® Historical*

*Available in the series romance section,
or in the historical romance section,
wherever books are sold.*

**We'll be spotlighting a different series
every month throughout 2009
to celebrate our 60th anniversary.**

Look for Harlequin® Historical in May!

Celebrations begin with
a sumptuous Regency house party!

Join three scandalous sisters in

**THE DIAMONDS OF
WELBOURNE MANOR**

Glittering, scintillating, sensual fun
by Diane Gaston, Deb Marlowe
and Amanda McCabe.

**60 years of Harlequin,
600 years of romance
in Harlequin Historical!**

Silhouette®

Desire

MAN of the MONTH

LEANNE BANKS

BILLIONAIRE EXTRAORDINAIRE

Billionaire Damien Medici is determined to get revenge on his enemy, but his buttoned-up new assistant Emma Weatherfield has been assigned to spy on him and might thwart his plans. As tensions in and out of the boardroom heat up, he convinces her to give him the information he needs—by getting her to unbutton a few things....

**Available May
wherever books are sold.**

REQUEST YOUR FREE BOOKS!

2 FREE NOVELS PLUS 2 FREE GIFTS!

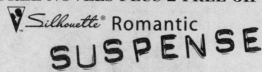

Silhouette® Romantic SUSPENSE

Sparked by Danger, Fueled by Passion!

YES! Please send me 2 FREE Silhouette® Romantic Suspense novels and my 2 FREE gifts (gifts are worth about $10). After receiving them, if I don't wish to receive any more books, I can return the shipping statement marked "cancel." If I don't cancel, I will receive 4 brand-new novels every month and be billed just $4.24 per book in the U.S. or $4.99 per book in Canada. That's a savings of at least 15% off the cover price! It's quite a bargain! Shipping and handling is just 25¢ per book*. I understand that accepting the 2 free books and gifts places me under no obligation to buy anything. I can always return a shipment and cancel at any time. Even if I never buy another book from Silhouette, the two free books and gifts are mine to keep forever.

240 SDN EEX6   340 SDN EEYJ

Name	(PLEASE PRINT)	
Address		Apt. #
City	State/Prov.	Zip/Postal Code

Signature (if under 18, a parent or guardian must sign)

Mail to the **Silhouette Reader Service:**
IN U.S.A.: P.O. Box 1867, Buffalo, NY 14240-1867
IN CANADA: P.O. Box 609, Fort Erie, Ontario L2A 5X3

Not valid to current subscribers of Silhouette Romantic Suspense books.

Want to try two free books from another line?
Call 1-800-873-8635 or visit www.morefreebooks.com.

* Terms and prices subject to change without notice. Prices do not include applicable taxes. Sales tax applicable in N.Y. Canadian residents will be charged applicable provincial taxes and GST. Offer not valid in Quebec. This offer is limited to one order per household. All orders subject to approval. Credit or debit balances in a customer's account(s) may be offset by any other outstanding balance owed by or to the customer. Please allow 4 to 6 weeks for delivery. Offer available while quantities last.

Your Privacy: Silhouette is committed to protecting your privacy. Our Privacy Policy is available online at www.eHarlequin.com or upon request from the Reader Service. From time to time we make our lists of customers available to reputable third parties who may have a product or service of interest to you. If you would prefer we not share your name and address, please check here. ☐

You're invited to join our Tell Harlequin Reader Panel!

By joining our new reader panel you will:

- Receive Harlequin® books—they are FREE and yours to keep with no obligation to purchase anything!
- Participate in fun online surveys
- Exchange opinions and ideas with women just like you
- Have a say in our new book ideas and help us publish the best in women's fiction

In addition, you will have a chance to win great prizes and receive special gifts!
See Web site for details. Some conditions apply.
Space is limited.

To join, visit us at
www.TellHarlequin.com.

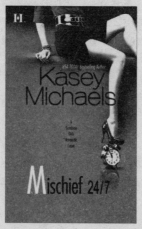

Harlequin® Historical
Historical Romantic Adventure!

If you enjoyed reading
Joanne Rock in the
Harlequin® Blaze™ series,
look for her new book
from Harlequin® Historical!

THE KNIGHT'S RETURN
Joanne Rock

Missing more than his memory,
Hugh de Montagne sets out to find his
true identity. When he lands in a small
Irish kingdom and finds a new liege in the
Irish king, his hands are full with his new
assignment: guarding the king's beautiful,
exiled daughter. Sorcha has had her heart
broken by a knight in the past. Will she be
able to open her heart to love again?

Available April
wherever books are sold.

Romantic
SUSPENSE

COMING NEXT MONTH

Available April 28, 2009

#1559 LADY KILLER—Kathleen Creighton
The Taken
When Tony Whitehall is enlisted to find out more about
Brooke Fallon Grant, who's accused of murdering her abusive ex-husband,
she insists that she—and her pet cougar, Lady—are
innocent. Sparks fly between Tony and Brooke as they try to save
the animal's life and discover who the killer really is.

#1560 HIS 7-DAY FIANCÉE—Gail Barrett
Love in 60 Seconds
Starting a new life in Las Vegas, Amanda Patterson never predicted she'd
be assaulted by a gunman in a casino. Owner Luke Montgomery fears bad
publicity and convinces her to keep quiet. When someone tries to kidnap
her daughter, Amanda agrees to Luke's plan to temporarily move in with
him and act as his fiancée, but their growing attraction soon puts them all
in danger.

#1561 NIGHT RESCUER—Cindy Dees
H.O.T. Watch
Wracked with survivor's guilt, former Special Forces agent
John Hollister agrees to put his suicide on hold to deliver medical
researcher Melina Montez to the mountains of Peru. As sexual heat and
desire flare, she reveals the fatal mission she's on to rescue her family,
and together they challenge each other to fight to stay alive for love.

#1562 HIGH-STAKES HOMECOMING—Suzanne McMinn
Haven
Intending to lay claim to his inherited family farm, Penn Ramsey is
shocked to discover the woman who once broke his heart. Willa also
claims the farm is hers, and when a storm strands them at the house
together, they discover their attraction hasn't died and all isn't as it seems.
Is the house trying to keep them from leaving? Or is something—or
someone—else at work here?

SRSCNMBPA0409